Telling Tales

by

Dick Wild

Grosvenor House
Publishing Limited

This book is published by
Grosvenor House Publishing Ltd
28-30 High Street, Guildford, Surrey, GU1 3EL.
www.grosvenorhousepublishing.co.uk

A CIP record for this book
is available from the British Library

ISBN 978-1-78148-744-0

Foreword

A fourth collection of short stories...

Drawn from a range of situations....

Encompassing a range of styles....

Aimed at anyone with an eye for a simple tale – and without the need to be too uplifted by the things they read!!

DW

Contents

Bartholomew's Toy

'What is it?' asked the bespectacled boy perched cross-legged on the lounge floor and reaching for the parcel being handed to him by his mother – his father hovering close enough to bear witness to the scene about to unfold. His wife hesitated.

'Well, why not open it and see.' She hesitated again, casting optimistic glances at both her husband peering cautiously over her shoulder and the gaudy coloured packaging about to be rent asunder before both their gazes.

At the invitation the boy – Bartholomew, the couple's seven year-old son – tore into the gaily decorated red and white paper, flinging its shreds aside to reveal the lid of a shiny cardboard box with illustrations of tiny animals and green and brown mauve patterns splashed across it, attempting to make what he could of the pictures and the words printed around them.

An opportune moment for his mother to step in – allowing him the privilege of lifting the lid but on-hand to answer whatever questions would likely arise.

'It's a farm!' she announced, eager to get things off on what she hoped was a positive footing, sharing the boy's eye skirting the box's contents before reaching for a plastic square-looking thing with a slope protruding from its top.

'What does it do?' asked the boy, no less puzzled than before the unveiling.

'Well – let's see.' His mother spread her arms and shifted herself closer.

'That's the farmhouse,' said his father, taking his place at his wife's side.

'Where the farmer and his wife live,' explained his wife.

1

'And their two children...'

'And a few dogs and cats...'

'What do *they* do?' asked the boy at once. His mother reached to the tray lifting pieces from two of the remaining slots in the plastic base.

'Well let's see,' said his mother, indicating their son should follow suit – helping himself to more of the contents wrapped in cellophane, in his case turning them a few times and rattling them close to his ear before returning to the plastic box, turning it upside down to view it from an alternative angle and check for any goodies like chocolate buttons about to drop into his lap.

'It's a nice big house,' said his father. 'With lots of rooms.'

'And a nursery for their little baby that will be arriving soon.' His mother folded a hand in an arc from her midriff as illustration of future developments.

The boy put the box to one side, turning his attention to a number of smaller packages still occupying the slots round the one reserved for the farmhouse.

'That's the farmer,' said his mother, observing the plastic cover being wrenched away and the figure extended at arm's length. 'He toils all day long, tending to the animals and working in the fields.'

'Driving the tractor,' said his father.

'So he can dig up all the crops of wheat and barley.'

'To sell at the market.'

'And feed his family.'

The boy made a closer examination of the plastic figure dressed in a floppy-looking hat and blue overalls and wearing a broad smile.

'And that's his wife,' added his mother watching a second figure being removed from its polythene protection. She wore a blue dress and had long brown hair, her arms held by her sides.

Which was the moment to step in once again – taking the plastic figure from her son's grasp and showing him how to ease the arms back and forth, up and down. In the case of the farmer's wife – reaching for pans to make a nice stew for the family's supper. And…in the case of her husband – extending one foot in front of the other to make his way to the barn to tend to his bales of hay or sit in his tractor to set off digging the earth to grow potatoes and turnips.

'And…' It was his mother's turn to reach in the box to lift two smaller figures lying side by side next to the slot for the tractor.

'Susan, their six-year-old daughter.'

'And her twelve-year-old brother – John.'

The introductions done it was time to step back, giving the boy a minute or two to come to terms with his new possession, allowing him to unwrap the remaining figures and pop them back and forth on the carpet and wheel the tractor round the field a few times.

Following their retreat to the kitchen the boy obligingly turned his attention to the remaining contents of the box: a brace of cows, three sheep and the family's cat and dog – all placed on the carpet alongside the farmer and a big red tractor complete with rubber wheels and a seat for the farmer to sit on.

Which seemed to be about it! And on initial inspection left him feeling somewhat at a loss. Things moved and twisted and you could wheel the red thing that looked a bit like a tank up and down the carpet. But beyond that there seemed little to get excited about. Not one of them seemed capable of wielding a machete or firing a Kalashnikov rifle or operating a sub-machine gun or an AK 47 from the floor of an abandoned building. Or firing arrows back and forth across the settee in a last-ditch defence against an advancing cavalry. Or even firing a pea-shooter – traditionally sellotaped to a bar of chocolate as a Christmas gift from his Great Aunt Hilda and her sister Alice.

Quite how anyone was expected to occupy himself for any length of time with a few plastic figures and a dog and cat, and a box with a lid was anybody's guess. He scoured the scene for possibilities he might yet have overlooked.

'Anything happening?' Her husband was calling from the kitchen where he was tipping milk into two cups and placing biscuits on each saucer.

'He's just looking at the moment,' said his wife, following proceedings through a crack in the door.

'Here.' A cup was handed to her as she turned from the door. 'Your turn.' She stepped aside to let her husband settle against the wall and lean into the edge of the door, enabling him to take her place.

'I think he's got hold of one of the cows,' he said.

'And_____' His wife was stood at his side.

'Don't know.' He leant further, his forehead nestled against the jamb of wood. 'I think he might be introducing it to the farmer's wife.'

Her husband squinted to get a better angle. 'Now it's one of the sheep...being introduced to one of the cows.' Nursing her mug, his wife stepped back, making her way to the door, urging her husband to follow.

'Come on, let's get back and show him how things work and what actually goes on.'

They resumed their positions, not wishing to be seen as interfering but keen to fill him in on whatever details sprang to mind to enable him to get the most out of his new toy.

Seated cross-legged and positioned as close to the action as was feasible, his mother took the farmer in hand, having him hop...hop...hop his way towards the farmhouse.

'See – the farmer, whose name is Giles, is going inside where his wife has got dinner on the table...'

'After his long day working in the fields...' said his father, reaching across.

Farmer Giles was brought hop...hop...hopping to the door where the dog and cat were waiting to be brought onto the scene. And within seconds the door was open.

4

'See...in goes the farmer.' A twist of his arms had them raised to horizontal position to greet his wife.

'And – the cat wants to be let in too.'

'Now – here's the farmer's wife...Mrs Giles.' A quick manoeuvre had her arms out ready to greet her husband, the greeting taking place in the hall just before making their way to the kitchen to start serving up tea.

'Now...' His mother shuffled closer reaching inside the raised roof of the house to have the farmer's wife Mrs. Giles take up her position by the cooker. 'A nice hot meal and then they'll all gather round the fire and tell each other stories.' Both dog and cat were lifted from the door and placed by the fire where they immediately curled up by the hearth and fell asleep.

'But first, the farmer needs to go and check outside.'

'He thinks he might have heard a strange noise,' said his mother.

'A fox?' Bartholomew suggested. His mother thought a minute.

'No...' She thought a little longer___

'The wind blowing in the barn,' said her husband, quickly steering the farmer in the direction of the big brown building in the yard.

'Open...shut...open...shut.' His mother had taken hold of the barn, easing its door open and shut a few times in return for Bartholomew paying close enough attention to step in and open and close the door himself – getting him used to operating one of the toy's key features.

'Maybe it was a fox hiding behind the door till the farmer's gone, waiting to creep out and get the chickens,' he suggested, quickly slamming the door shut should a fox or some other predator still be skulking around inside.

'Oh I don't know about that,' said his mother, trot...trot... trotting them all back across the farmyard and into the farmhouse. Opportunity for her husband to take the tractor on a final spin round the yard before putting it to bed for the night next to the sheep and cows.

'What they do is – use the tractor to take the eggs to market,' said his father

'And take milk to the milkman,' said his wife lifting Mrs. Giles from her place by the cooker.

'Because – apart from working on the farm, digging the fields and feeding the animals they have to get things ready for the new baby.' His mother made a second arc-shape with her hand.

'A little boy,' said his father.

'What about if it's a girl?' said Bartholomew.

'It won't be a girl,' said his mother.

'How do you know?' said the boy.

'Well – they just know.'

'She's had a scan,' said his father quickly. 'And when he's older, the boy will learn to drive the tractor,' he added, deftly avoiding the look he was getting from a few feet away.

'And one day he'll have a farm of his own with lots of animals.'

'And a family of his own.'

'And they'll go for walks in the country.'

'And the children will play on the tractor.'

'And granny and grandad will come and ride round the farm with them on the tractor.'

'And then they'll all go inside and have a nice cup of tea and a slice of cake,' said her husband making steering-wheel shapes with his hands.

'They'd be too old to ride the tractor,' said Bartholomew, quick to seize on any potential flaw in proceedings. 'They might fall out and go under its wheels.'

'Oh I don't think so,' said his mother, casting another glance at her husband.

'And after tea they'll sit round the fire and talk.'

'And then take granny and granddad back home in the car.'

Which was the moment for the pair to launch themselves once more to their feet. There was a lot to take in and the last thing they wanted was to give the boy too much information at one sitting. And – just like the farmer and his wife – they were going to get tea ready and in twenty minutes they too would be sitting round the table just like the farmer's family, telling each other what they'd been up to and asking the children what they'd learnt at school that day.

They made their exit, trot...trot...trotting their way back to the kitchen to set about preparing their evening meal.

Behind them the boy's curiosity was beginning to wane. He tried rotating the plastic figures, shuffling them back and forth and up and down the farmhouse walls SAS-style; taking one of the sheep to inspect its hind quarters, sniffing it and raising it to eye level – aiming its tiny black snout at the tv set and pulling on one of its legs in imitation of a trigger effect – but alas to no avail.

A swift upending of the farmhouse followed – a more expedient means of getting at the kids; trot...trot...trotting them outside for a quick spin on the tractor, having it perform a few wheelies round the yard, then abandoning it to chase each other round the back of the barn with sticks before collapsing in a heap and in the time-honoured act of conciliation – slotting together like jig-saw pieces behind bales of hay.

All pretty tame stuff. With mounting frustration he continued to survey the scene, his eye eventually settling on the huge metal fortress of an insulated fire-guard.

And immediately thinking he might just have the answer....

Steadying himself, the instruction arrived from HQ: a last-ditch retreat from a wave of scud-missile attacks from behind enemy lines....

Easing the guard to one side a hand reached across making a grab for the cluster of figures: the farmer, his wife and the two children – each launched, one by one, into the heart of the fire where they bounced and jostled for position before wilting and finally combusting into a line of tiny flames – as effective a display of miniature napalm as could be imagined.

The only survivor – a fox, last spotted skulking suspiciously next to a line of dead chickens.

'How's he doing?' came the cry from the kitchen. Some feet away, her husband settled himself to focus through the crack in the door.

'Not sure,' he said, adjusting his stance to get a better view. 'But I think something might be happening.'

Tom's Double-Whammy

Thomas Ormrod had a thing about small packages arriving in the post. He would take his time ordering them, sometimes well in advance, then sit patiently, day after day waiting for the flap of the letter-box, the plop on the hall-carpet or ring at the front door bell if it was one of his larger purchases. His wife – Gladys Ormrod – though not exactly amused, was inclined to turn a blind eye. She knew men and compared to the antics of some of the blokes she could name, it was all relatively harmless.

It was a bright April morning but chilly with it. The sun was beginning to find its feet but only just. Thomas Ormrod was in his chair seeking something to get him through the first few hours of the day. It often worked out like this first thing after breakfast – sitting in his chair unable to settle on anything. He'd read a bit of the paper, listen to a bit of radio, watch his wife busying herself in out, in out, then maybe get out in the kitchen himself to put the kettle on.

It was as he flicked the switch to bring the kettle to the boil that the flip of the letter-box announced the arrival of the day's post. There was something about the sound of that 'plop' on the hall-carpet that had him abandoning the kettle for a minute.

It was with some glee that he leant to pick up a small brown parcel off the floor in front of the door, checking a few details and whipping it into the living-room to put it to one side for a minute to go and get his cup of tea. There was something to be said for delaying the opening of parcels till you've a cup of tea at hand.

Back in his chair, he reached across, re-examining the post mark on the front and tearing open the packaging.

He'd spotted this one in one of his more frequently visited periodicals, the 'Advertiser's Market-Place' which specialised in easily-affordable, across-the-board ideas for all ages... guaranteed to *'bring a smile – every time – whatever the occasion.'* Some of the stuff they'd got in there was unbelievable, especially the special-offers. If you took your time, checking the fine print and comparing prices, by and large you couldn't go wrong.

He finished removing the layer of packaging and lifted the two flaps of a small cardboard box, brushing a bit of paper aside and lifting the pseudo-silver lid and chain from its place in the tissue lining.

He let the watch hang from its chain for a moment, extending it at arm's length and then reaching to release the catch.

With a flip the lid dropped, revealing a strikingly clear miniature of Saddam Hussein, the Iraqi dictator, posed against a bright scarlet surround. Back to the catch he flicked it a second time. A second lid dropped – Osama-Bin-Laden, the Al-Qaeda leader popping into view, in this case cast against a sharp turquoise background.

Assured that once again he'd managed to come up trumps he closed the lid to repeat the procedure: first flick...Saddam Hussein, surrounded by what, on closer inspection proved to be a scarlet tinted sky. Second flick – Osama-Bin-Laden peering benevolently from what proved to be streaks of emerald/turquoise sky. Each time – same result: Saddam Hussein – Osama-Bin-Laden. Seven times he repeated the process before clasping the cover shut and brushing the bits of packaging to one side.

The return of his wife from the shops was the signal to rise from his chair and follow her into the kitchen.

She was in the process of removing packets and tins from her bag and popping them on the counter when he appeared behind her.

She stopped unloading the bag.

He waited till he had her attention before hoisting the watch to view, the silver chain dangling a few inches in front of her face. Flipping the lid he presented her with her first glimpse of Saddam Hussein, jigging him up and down to add to the effect. 'Saddam Hussein,' he said. Then had her watch again as, with a second flip of a lid, Osama-Bin-Laden sprang into view. 'Osama-Bin-Laden.' He quickly closed the lid and opened it again, watching with her, still nudging the chain. 'Saddam Hussein.' Quick flick of the lid…'Osama-Bin-Laden.'

His wife turned to put a two-pound bag of sugar and tins of beans in the cupboard, closing the cabinet door and turning to the sink.

Thomas closed the lid and stepped back to avoid getting under his wife's feet, and to give Osama-Bin-Laden a more thorough viewing, again holding the watch at length.

His wife shifted him again to get to the pots and pans in the cupboard. Thomas closed the lid and flicked it again, directing it at the rear of his wife's head…'Saddam Hussein.' He looked again at the matchbox-size portraits. On closer inspection, one could conceivably be the other's dad. Father and son…a double-whammy!

He stepped aside to let his wife past, on this occasion making his way back in the living room where, once settled in the chair, he reached for the accompanying leaflet, working his way through the fine print. *Double-Flick; Double-Face, Duo-Watch-Wonder.* Distributed from *O.A. Optic Novelties, Luton Beds.*

Two hours later, there was a spring in the step of Thomas Ormrod as he stepped from his door to begin the fifteen minute schlep to his local pub *The Red Lion.*

With the watch placed firmly in his pocket, he stepped over the threshold and made his way toward the bar-room regulars already ensconced on their stools: Alf Eccles, a local plasterer. To his right, Sam, a local gardener and a bit of a comic who made a point of rowing with his missus in public every now and then just to make it clear neither of them was into any of this lovey-dovey bollocks.

"right Tom.' Tom nodded and made his way across the floor.

"Right Sam,' he said, casting a nod at the others – Albert and Jud watching Tom's arrival, Sam conjuring up some jovial observation to get them off on the right foot, Jud saddled with his involuntary (though some weren't so sure about this) squint that sometimes made him appear to be winking when in fact he wasn't: a liability on occasions, particularly with some of the younger women who didn't know quite what to make of him and were inclined to give him a wide berth at the bar. Maybe on account of his squint, he had a tendency to be the last to stand his round, particularly during evening sessions when you could blow a fortune with everyone and his dog appearing on the scene.

Tom took his pint of *Fosters*, sipping his way through the layer of foam.

'What yer up to?' said Sam, watching as Tom placed the glass on the bar and made for his pocket.

Raising a smile Tom drew his hand from his pocket.

'Watch,' he said, grasping the chain and dangling the watch at arm's length. All eyes were on him as he raised it to view and had it complete its first trick, flicking open the lid.

'Saddam Hussein,' he said, holding it a moment to have them take note. Eyes waited for the second flip. 'Osama-Bin-Laden.'

The men were intrigued, whether impressed or not, would be difficult to gauge as yet. Each took hold of his glass.

"s alright that, innit,' said Sam nodding.

Tom flexed the chain, bobbing Bin-Laden up and down a few times to bring a bit of life to his somewhat lacklustre expression.

'Who is it? said Albert, leaning for a better look. All eyes – some jovial, some quizzical – turned on him.

'Bin-Laden,' said Sam with a nod at Tom's watch. 'Fuckin' Al-Qaeda guy.'

Tom clasped it shut and repeated the process, demonstrating the ease of the operation.

Geoff the barman, a gruff individual who took exception to people complaining about the beer, pulled a few dribs and drabs from the *Theakstons* spout into a waiting glass.

'What you got there then Tom?' he said grounding the glass. Tom swung the chain in his direction and clasped the lid shut. With an eye fixed on the watch he flicked the lid.

'Saddam Hussein,' he said, holding the contraption close enough for Geoff to get full view. 'Osama-Bin-Laden.' He flicked the inner clasp, revealing the less avuncular features of the Al Qaeda leader. Geoff watched, flicking the lever of the *Guinness* tap for Gee, another regular whose day consisted of plonking himself on the same stool in the same corner from opening time till dusk and drinking the black-stuff – and only the black-stuff – as he liked to remind everyone at regular intervals – until such time as the glasses' contents had done its trick sufficiently to head him off into the night, resolved, as he again liked to remind everyone at regular intervals, that with his day complete, he was about to go home and make his wife's evening complete.

'Where d'you get that then Tom?' Geoff asked. Tom closed the lid and gave it a few wipes with his sleeve.

'*Post. O.A. Optics, Luton.*' He still had the chain held tight in his grip.

"s alright innit,' said Geoff.

'What did it cost you then Tom?' said Jud.

'Not much,' said Tom, drawing chain and watch into the palm of his hand.

A figure approached from a corner table – a bespectacled individual with bushy eyebrows and a shock of wiry platinum hair. He stood a moment, glass in hand, contemplating the implications of going the whole hog and actually grabbing the barman's attention. Geoff watched his approach, stiffening at the sight of a virtually full pint raised to view between them.

The regulars turned to watch. It was a familiar routine but one worth observing all the same. The man eyed the glass's contents – coughing before he spoke.

'I think it might be the end of the barrel,' he said, stirring the flaccid contents as hopefully sufficient evidence. Geoff gave the glass a quick glance and huffed a little, the others looking on with some amusement. Being strictly lager-men, there was always mileage to be had in checking out the antics of these beer drinkers. The man shook the glass as further demonstration.

'What's up with it?' said Geoff, adopting his customary stance that intimated anyone complaining about the beer was in-effect taking liberties. The man re-shook the glass, strands of what looked like mini-plankton shimmering in the base.

'Well, it's a bit appley and a bit flat. I just thought it might be towards the end of the barrel.' They watched Geoff take the glass and hold it to the light.

'Appley?…Looks all right to me.'

'Well it's got that appley edge, like it's maybe on the turn. So I just thought I'd mention it,' said the man, his voice dropping in quiet acknowledgment of yet another case of people in the trade knowing nothing or caring little about the product they sold to earn a living. Geoff scowled and aimed the glass at the sink.

'Ale's like that,' he said finally, discarding the contents with a grimace.

The man, breathing a little more easily at seeing the glass's contents dispatched without further discussion, laid two hands on the bar and ran his eye along the remaining pumps. Geoff placed the glass behind him.

'I'll give yer another pint, but there's nowt wrong with it,' he said, vindicated in having the last say, whatever the outcome. The man pointed to an end pump when asked what he wanted instead. Geoff pulled the pint and handed the glass over without giving a thought to its contents. The man had already decided it would be a marked improvement. Geoff was back to his pint of *Becks*, downing a third of it in one go.

'Beer a bit iffy?' said Alf.

'Fuck-all wrong with it,' said Geoff.

'Stick to *Guinness*,' came the cry from the corner, his glass half raised. No-one seemed inclined to argue.

A youngish couple, Andy and his wife Cheryl entered. There were looks at the bar; Sam swore. Andy and Cheryl went everywhere and did everything together. Rumour had it they even played board-games together in the evenings. Which wasn't to say there was anything wrong with that, it was just a bit odd and made Sam feel like swearing whenever they came in the pub.

'Pint of *Fosters*,' said Andy, his voice extending across the seated figures. 'Cheese&Onion crisps.'

'Cider?' asked Geoff reaching for a second glass.

'Please,' confirmed Cheryl, rooting around in her bag.

"Right Tom,' said Andy.

'What you got there then Tom?' asked Cheryl, eyeing something silvery-looking being juggled in the palm of Tom's hand.

Tom dangled the watch-chain in front of Cheryl and then in front of the pair of them once Andy had finished placing his order at the bar.

He waited till they were ready, holding the silver lid at arm's length.

'Watch,' said Tom. They watched the lid flip. 'Saddam Hussein.' The pair eyed the largely indecipherable features peering from the scarlet surround. He flipped a second lid. 'Osama-Bin-Laden.'

Andy sipped his *Fosters* and reached for his packet of Cheese&Onion crisps. Cheryl leant to examine the face more closely.

'Looks like Jesus with a beard,' she said, straightening herself on the stool.

'Where d'you get it?' asked Andy.

'*O.A Optics, Luton*,' said Tom, gathering the chain and watch back in the palm of his hand and holding them there a moment. He reached for his glass. Andy nodded, Sam drank his *Budweiser* and sneezed. His hayfever was back, not aided by drinking *Budweiser* by all accounts.

'Dead in't he?' said Alf.

'Who?'

'Bin-Laden.' There were nods on all sides.

'Yanks got him last year.'

'Shot 'im.'

'Then chucked 'im over a boat.'

'That's 'cause 'e was a Muslim. You got to get rid of 'em quick.'

'Cos the sun gets to 'em,' said Alf.

'Pint of *4X* Geoff,' said Sam, leaning over what little space at the bar remained. Geoff moved a glass to the tap and flicked the lever.

'Hussein's dead too,' said Jud observing Albert trying to get a grip on the American football game on *Sky*.

'Who's winning then Albert?' he asked in typically droll fashion, his voice lofted above the heads that separated them.

'Fuck knows,' said Albert, planting his glass on the bar, eyes turned to the screen.

'I thought he looked quite sad when they dug him out the cellar,' said Cheryl.

'Who?' said Sam.'

'Saddam Hussein. When they found him and brought him out of the cellar – his hair, his beard; he looked a bit trampy, not that I've anything against tramps,' she added placing her glass on the bar and reaching for her purse.

'Gentlemen-of-the-road,' said Alf, glass raised and taking another quick swig of his *4X*.

'Anyone else want a drink?' asked Cheryl seeking to change the subject, looking round in time to spot Jud – arm raised – the other emptying the contents of his glass with a hefty swig.

'He'd been hiding,' said Sam.

'Hiding from the Yankees,' said Alf.

Albert abandoned the screen to check for any bits swimming round in his pint of *Fosters*.

Gee, usually one for minding his own business in the corner, was wobbling a bit. He'd been on the razz till one, back to his mate's house to carry on there and been up till dawn. All he'd had was a bacon-sarni and a cup of tea.

'Let's 'ave another look Tom,' he mumbled, indicating Tom should hand the gadget over for closer inspection. Tom was off his seat and round the bar.

'What is it?' said Gee, making every effort to re-focus on the contraption dangling from Tom's wrist.

'Watch,' said Tom, holding the watch steady and flicking the catch, letting the lid drop. 'Saddam Hussein.' Watching again as the second lid dropped. 'Osama-Bin-Laden.'

Gee looked closer and immediately stiffened on his stool, reaching for his glass which, unbeknown to him, had reduced itself to a few creamy black dribbles. Tom clasped the lid, rubbed its chrome surface a few times against his sleeve and returned to his stool.

'He was a cunt,' Gee shouted after him, offering the observation as an afterthought and wavering even more unsteadily on his stool.

The door opened and three girls (or women) in their late teens entered. Albert and Jud broke from the American football for a moment and caught Alf's eye.

'Your Hayley Alf – and her friends.' There was some delay over the announcement. Alf's daughter's friends had a knack of slowing conversation a little.

'Vodka tonics?' said Geoff, quick to tend to the girls and already reaching for the appropriate glasses. Nods followed – Alf's daughter, Hayley, struggling to find her way through her purse.

'Oh, where've I put it. Don't tell me I've left it at home.'

She stopped and shuffled up to her father.

'Dad, lend us a tenner, when we get back I'll give it you straight back. I've got it upstairs in a drawer in my dressing table.' She looked him in the eye and gripped his hand.

'Fuck off,' he said.

'Oh dad.'

She burrowed back inside the bag, rearranging its contents and muttering to herself.

Her father raised his glass, turning to Jud whose wink seemed to have stepped up a gear at the arrival of Alf's daughters' friends. It was difficult to keep abreast of what was happening at times.

'You get that ceiling done in the end?' he said.

'Yeh, just about,' said Jud. 'Pain in the arse though.'

'Pain in the arse ceilings,' said Geoff from across the counter.

'It's okay – I've found it,' said Hayley, snapping the bag shut and waving a ten-pound note at her friends. 'I knew I'd got it.' She looked at her father. 'It's alright dad, I've got it.'

Her father made a point of checking the state-of-play in the ball-game. 'Who's winning then Albert?' he asked, seeking further routes into distracting Albert's attention. Albert shrugged. Despite following proceedings for the last fifteen minutes or so, it was still mostly noodles to him. 'Fuck knows,' he said. There were chuckles on both sides of the bar.

Tom had taken the watch from his pocket and was dangling it loosely in the direction of the girls. Simone, one of Hayley's friends, was first to notice.

'What's that?' she asked, genuinely curious and leaning over her friend's shoulder. Tom raised his hand, jigging the chain in her direction.

'Watch,' he said. Simone and Kathy watched him take the silver chain and extend it. Watching too as he flipped the lid and held it in their direction.

'Saddam Hussein,' he said. Then watching again as he flipped the lid a second time.

'Osama-Bin-Laden,' he said, rotating the watch face a second time, enabling them all to get a decent view. The girls looked on.

'Looks like Aladdin,' said Simone.

'How much it cost?' asked Tina, Hayley and Simone's friend.

'Not much,' said Tom.

There was a shout and a clap of hands at the bar, all eyes turned on the screen.

'What's happening?' said Alf.

'Touchdown!..Tennessee Titons!' said Jud.

'Where d'you get it?' asked Hayley, her attention still on Tom's watch.

'*O A Optic Novelties, Luton,*' said Tom replacing the lid.

'Who d'you say it is?' asked Tina. Tom pushed the watch in her direction, flicking the two lids in turn.

'Saddam Hussein...Osama-Bin-Laden.' Tina took a drink of her vodka-tonic, eyeing Bin-Laden who appeared to be giving her the eye from his turquoise sky background.

'Have a go,' said Tom handing the watch across, prepared to let Tina or her friend flip the lid herself. Simone shared the viewing with Tina and Carol who'd been watching from over Simone's shoulder, finally taking it from Tina's grasp.

'What do I do?' asked Carol, searching for indication as to how to release the lid. Tom pointed out the tiny button. 'Just flip it,' he said.

Carol flipped the lid once, twice, jumping slightly as the second lid fell from its slot.

'Who is it?' she asked

'Bin-Laden,' said Tom. 'Osama-Bin-Laden.' He strained forwards, eyeing the figure in a little more detail.

'Al-Qaeda guy,' said Jud from his stool, taking a hefty swig of *Fosters* and returning to the screen.

'Deceased!' added Albert.

It was Andy's round.

'When you're ready Geoff.' Geoff nodded, placing glasses on the stands and flicking a few levers.

'Geoff.' Gee called from his corner, picking up on the replenishment of glasses, his own glass hovering in the air.

'Alright Gee.' Geoff looked to the *Fosters* tap and flicked the lever, reaching simultaneously for the *Guinness* lever.

Hayley and Simone sipped vodkas and turned to the screen. 'What's on?' asked Simone.

'Tennessee Titons,' said Jud.

'Tina, do you want a drink?' Hayley was looking back at her friend from the bar.

'What I want to know is – what you got 'im for?' A voice rang out from across the bar – Gee intent on pursuing the issue of Tom's recently-acquired possession in light of it seeming to be the centre of everyone's attention. 'He's a fuckin' wanker.' He'd succeeded in straightening himself on his stool and was offering the observations to anyone who happened to be within earshot. 'They both were.'

The door opened, admitting Meryl, mid-thirties, maybe late thirties, it was difficult to say: her plaster-cast appearance as impeccable as her approach to life, fastidious and totally un-compromising. With Meryl – what you saw was what you got.

She wasted no time in getting herself to the bar and placing her order whilst shaking her purse to rescue some of the loose change that was apt to gather in droves and really wind her up.

'White wine and soda Geoff.' She failed to look up to where Geoff already had the glass poised beneath the optic.

'Alright Meryl?' said Sam taking a swig of *Budweiser* and watching her clasp the purse shut.

'Ask me tomorrow,' said Meryl. 'Or better still – next week.' She flung the handbag over her shoulder. 'That's fine,' she said, responding to Geoff's triple squirt of soda into the chunks of ice. 'I can't be doing with this weather. Thanks Geoff,' she said. She drank thirstily and acknowledged a few looks. 'Sam, Jud.'

'Yes!' Another touch-down, Tennessee-Titons.

Tom waited for the moment to pass before withdrawing the watch from his pocket and making it visible as and when Meryl chose to look in his direction.

'What's happened?' said Meryl, distracted by Jud's exclama-tion.

'Tennessee-Titons, two down,' said Jud.

There was further exasperation at failing to find a tissue that she was sure she'd put in her bag. Tom jiggled the watch a little closer.

She'd found the tissue but as often with Meryl the air of impatience seemed to linger long after whatever had prompted it.

'What you got there Tom?' she asked, prepared to relent at seeing Tom brandishing something dangling from a chain. Tom waited till she'd finished blowing into the tissue.

'Watch,' he said, waiting for her to look up before letting the lid drop. 'Saddam Hussein...Osama-Bin-Laden.' She watched the second lid go the same way as the first, the turquoise sky behind Bin-Laden's head first thing to catch her eye. She gave it a moment but a disturbance just beneath her left eye was claiming her attention.

'Sorry Tom but I can't be doing with either of them I'm afraid.' She was busily peering into a pocket mirror, flicking her eye-lashes and dabbing repeatedly at a small blemish she'd discovered just above the cheekbone. 'I had a friend who was in Orlando when it all kicked-off. Said it was absolutely terrible – the worst thing ever!'

She stopped, replacing the mirror, eyes rolling, the lashes still proving an irritation by insisting on interlocking every time she blinked. 'I have to say, it's a bit of a strange thing to carry round with you Tom. Where did you get it?'

Tom closed and then opened the lids the third time in succession.

'O A Optics, Luton,' he said still staring at the lid before replacing it in his pocket.

'When what kicked-off?' said Alf, picking up the strands of the conversation from a few feet away.

'9/11,' said Meryl rolling her other eye. 'Twin-towers. My friends were in Orlando when it happened.' She stopped, widening both eyes to check for further interference. 'Said it was the worst thing – ever – bar nothing!' Alf took a drink of 4X.

'That weren't Saddam Hussein,' he said, seizing the opportunity to enlighten her a little.

'What wasn't?' the question came from over his shoulder.

'9/11.'

'It was Bin-Laden though,' said Sam, prepared to leap to Meryl's defence if only to liven things up a little.

'Well I'm sorry.' Meryl shook her head – clear indication of where she stood on the issue and absolving herself of further involvement. 'Bin-Laden, Saddam Hussein, I can't be doing with either of them.'

'Gassed his own people – The Kurds,' said Albert from the seat next to Alf.

'Who?'

'Hussein.'

'Yes, well – that's what I'm saying,' said Meryl. 'Anyway, don't get me on politics,' she added, eyes closed, chin and glass thrust defiantly in the direction of the bar. 'I can't be doing with it.'

'He was a cunt,' chipped in a voice from the corner, Gee just about capable of reminding everyone where he stood on the issue.

'Language Gee,' said Geoff, giving him a warning look. Gee's eyes wavered a little at the admonishment.

'Okay...arseole then. He was a fuckin'...arse'ole,' he said, quickly downing a third of his pint. 'They both were.'

The door opened and a figure in black turned to discard his cigarette butt before making his entry. It was Henry, a dour individual whose callow expression belied his thirty-nine, possibly forty years, and whose claim to fame was a knack for finding fault in just about everyone and everything who happened to come under his radar, and to present his reasons – often at considerable length – audience or no audience.

He walked in a lethargic stride, making straight for the bar, greeting the others with a curt nod of the head. His favoured pursuits, beyond finding fault with all and sundry, were smoking hand-rolled cigarettes, playing fruit machines – the licensed ones as opposed to the piddling excuses for machines stuck in the corners of pubs – and letting it be known (or reminding those who'd heard it before – like as not for the umpteenth time) that he was, as he liked to put it – 'his own man', in that he took no crap from anyone – never had and never would, thank you very much.

Slumped on his stool, he took the rum and coke and stared vaguely in the direction of the tv screen, just about able to make out it was American Football which was tailor-made for Americans on the grounds that they were a bunch of wankers. He shuffled his stool and set about getting ready for his next smoke, placing his *Golden Virginia* packet and papers on the bar, rolling the tobacco in the paper with just the right amount of pressure, nipping the end just so much as to stem a few wayward strands and keep the thing slim enough.

'Henry.' Acknowledgement came from Sam and briefly from Andy. A half nod for Cheryl, who he'd trust just about as far as he could chuck her, and who – for her part – regarded Henry as a pain-in-the-neck. His view – and one he'd occasionally share with the guys in private – was that she *needed* a pain – right up the fucking arse!

'Henry,' said Alf. Alf didn't have a lot of time for Henry either.

'Alf,' said Henry, who felt Alf too could be a pain in the arse as and when required.

'What you up to?' asked Jud, obliged to pop the question at finding himself stuck next to Henry at the bar.

Henry's profile rarely changed. 'This and that.' He fingered the end of his cigarette and put the packet to one side. 'Met a fella at the market the other day, offered us a job in town; small-time carpentry business down by the river. Offered me two-fifty a week. I told him bollocks.'

Jud switched his attention to the screen. It was job done as far as he, or anyone who found himself stuck next to Henry, was concerned. The trick was to get Henry in his place, rum-and-coke in front of him and retire unobtrusively from the scene. Few had qualms about leaving Henry to his own devices, certainly not Jud.

True to form, having completed the rolling of his cigarette Henry was getting into his stride – audience or no audience!

'I told him `you can fucking stick your two-fifty.` Fact is I don't work for two-fifty, not for no-one. I told him – What I do I do for myself. What I work for, is for *me*.'

A few seconds were devoted to tapping the end of the cigarette against the bar.

'I said you can stick your two-fifty. Kept his mouth shut after that.' The unlit cigarette was popped between his lips where it would hang limply until further notice.

Looking up to find his point made, at least for the time being, he observed Tom approaching, reaching for something in his pocket like he might be about to offer him some money. The arrival of a new face saw him prepared to change tack for a moment.

'What you got there?' He watched the silver lid and chain being drawn into Tom's hand.

'Watch,' said Tom, dangling the chain.

He quickly flicked the lid. 'Saddam Hussein.' He waited a moment and completed the second flip. 'Osama-Bin-Laden. He clamped it shut and ran through the manoeuvre a second time. Henry gave the miniatures a quick viewing.

'You nick it?'

'No, bought it. *O A Optics*, *Luton*,' said Tom.

'How much?'

'Not much.'

Henry shrugged. 'Fuckin' arse'oles, the pair of them.' An eye turned in the direction of the tv screen, the cigarette hanging limply from his lips. Tom was in the midst of another quick check on the watch's mechanism when a voice, slurred and semi-incoherent, rained in once again from across the bar.

'Tom!' Tom looked up to see Gee's arm extended in what at first hand could be construed as a gesture of celebration.

'Let's 'ave another look. Let's see it again.' The arm just about managed to remain in position, not to be retracted until the watch was presented for further inspection. Tom took the watch and placed himself next to Gee's stool.

'See,' he said, about to flip the lid to save Gee the aggravation of having to negotiate the procedure himself given the state he was in.

'No – give it 'ere.' His fingers beckoned, his body leaning to and fro, his eyes on the verge of closing. Tom reached across handing him the watch. Gee took it and gave its pseudo-silver lid a quick glance.

'How much?' he asked.

'Not much,' said Tom, watching Gee attempting to find the clasp to release the first of the two lids. Tom showed him where to press his finger and stood back.

'Where do you get it?' asked Gee.

'O A Optics, Luton,' said Tom, following Gee's repeated failure to release the catch. He stepped in, taking the watch, instantly springing Saddam Hussein into Gee's vision.

'Saddam Hussein,' he said, levelling the mini-portrait in Gee's direction. He released the second lid. 'Osama-Bin-laden,' he said, planting the watch in Gee's outstretched hand.

Gee wobbled and made an effort to focus on the, by now, largely indistinct features.

'Fuckin' arseoles – the pair of them,' he said finally, echoing Henry's observation and abandoning the attempt to focus on either of them, and by way of consolation – raising the watch in his hand and bringing it down with some force on the corner of the bar, a short splintering sound hard on the heels of the initial impact.

Heads turned as Gee raised what remained of the watch a second time, and brought it smashing down on the bar, splintering plastic and sending fragments of imitation silver skidding onto the floor.

'Fuckin' arse'oles,' he repeated, wobbling even more precariously and barely able to witness the scene of carnage he had wreaked on the area beneath his stool.

There were outbursts on all sides, accusations from Albert and Sam, both ready to leap into the fray on Tom's behalf. Even Henry, smoking his imaginary cigarette and eyeing the fragments littering the space around the stool, seemed somewhat taken-aback. 'They *were* a pair of wankers,' he said, adding the observation only after a moment's respite.

Alf and Cheryl had seen fit to join the communal gathering beneath Gee's stool. Geoff was quickly across, his tone clear indication of what was to follow.

'Enough Gee. Off you get. And I don't want to see you back for a while, okay.'

Gee rolled on his stool, his eyes rotating at the chaotic scenes that seemed to have erupted around him. Tom had himself been far from idle, scooping what bits of watch he could rescue from beneath Gee's stool and drawing himself back to his feet. Meryl looked across, words for once eluding her until Tom made a reappearance, bits of his watch clutched tightly in one hand.

'No – sorry Gee. You're out of order there. I can't be doing with that – smashing things just because you don't agree with it,' she said.

There was universal agreement. It was no way to carry on. Feelings – good, bad, or indifferent, even prompted by the likes of Saddam Hussein and Osama-Bin-Laden were not to be expressed in such a fashion as that. You didn't go around taking it out on a guy having a drink and minding his own business in the pub.

Even Gee, drawing himself unsteadily to his feet had hands raised aside semi-closed eyes – admission that perhaps he might have overstepped the mark a little, and turning with a declaration that it was indeed time to bid them all goodbye, and with his evening complete, get back home and – all things being equal – make his wife's evening complete.

'You alright there Tom?' Meryl watched as Tom gathered the bits and pieces of what remained of the watch and placed them on the bar.

Geoff appeared, armed with a bin for Tom to put the bits and pieces in.

'Where d'you get it Tom?' he asked, eager to be seen making the appropriate gestures.

'*O A Optics, Luton*', said Tom, reaching to lay the remnants of the watch to rest in the bin sitting on the bar.

'How much?'

'Not much.'

'Okay. Give us the details. We'll get another one ordered. Geoff already had the glass beneath the *Fosters* tap.

'On the house,' he said, placing the complimentary pint under Tom's nose.

Tom nodded.

'Yes!'

There was a moment's much-needed distraction around the tv screen.

'What's happening?' said Meryl, swinging round on her stool.

'Tennessee Vikings, another touchdown!' said Jud. Alf raised a glass and Jud clapped approval and winked at Tom who watched approvingly from his recently acquired stool.

'When you're ready Geoff,' came the cry from various quarters.

Mc Bain On The Subway

The entrance to the subway some thirty yards ahead was flanked by news-vendors, posters for up-and-coming Broadway musicals and a fleet of cars jammed to a standstill by a fleet of lights ahead. Oblivious to it all, Monica strode, head-bowed, shielded from the elements by a scarf, hat and thick second-hand coat and clutching a metal case that seemed strangely out of sorts – too big and too awkward to be wrestled along the sidewalk by a petite young woman with bouncing shoulder-length hair.

Case held slightly aloft, she filed her way down the steps, pausing only to check her footing on the grimy surface and sweep the scarf more firmly round her neck. The Cossack-style hat was pulled around her ears, effectively keeping her features hidden, which – on mornings such as this – seemed like an added bonus.

On arrival at the main concourse she made for the left hand side, weaving in and out of the steady entourage of traffic to what she now regarded as her patch of wall next to familiar posters for the city's Philharmonic and Jazz Ensemble Of New Jersey, whilst on the far side of the concourse, the barriers continued to hammer their own symphonic welcoming party to the trains headed for the Downtown destinations.

Having reached her spot, she grounded the case, stopping for a moment to breathe the cold sooty air and reach to her pocket for a key.

In her own time she reached to unlock the top catches and ease the shelf down. It was a neat enough contraption, picked up by a breaker's yard in Queens. At around eight feet in length, it was secured to the wall by means of a few bolts, the shelf able to drop and remain angled to enable it to be viewed from a distance.

She settled the legs of the stand and opened the case she had been carrying. Not all the books were taken home. The few older ones could be kept, secured behind the shelf's doors. The remaining space was filled with copies of more recent stuff – all-in-all a decent enough collection – varied and yet close enough to home and recent enough to maybe draw some attention.

As ever, her first move was to take a step back and then juggle the display – mixing more vibrant covers with the plainer ones, the bolder images juxtaposed against their more subtle counterparts. The facility to lower the shelf to a viewable angle was a definite plus, allowing a degree of independent browsing – something to bear in mind during the quieter moments.

Two placards had been laminated and backed against hardboard to be attached to an extension specially convened at the top of the stand. She'd toyed with what to put, aware of the need to draw some attention, yet wary of coming across as too pushy, eventually opting for *Monica's Subway Books*...as a simple enough starting-point, a few contact details included on the second board. A fold-up stool kept behind and locked with a cycle lock to a stanchion by the ticket barrier completed the scene.

All that remained at this time of day was coffee. She unclasped the lid of a small brown flask and poured the first of its tepid contents into the lid. It didn't taste too good, it never did, but it was comforting to grip something vaguely warm, the warmth spreading through her, helping convince her that her bid to bring a little color to life beneath the city's streets might not be entirely in vain.

She waited a moment, downing the remainder of the cup's contents and taking a swift overview of the shelf's contents lifted one of its opening contenders from the shelf. Having secured her favoured position on the right corner of the shelf, she extended the book, her voice raised to compete with the sounds of marching feet.

'*A Five Cents Hop From The Brooklyn Bridge.*'

The announcement drew a handful of blank looks.

'*A man searching for his estranged wife...*' She turned the book once, twice and held it again at arm's length.

'*...reveals secrets that he later finds may have been better kept secret...*'

An office worker and a woman, possibly his wife, looked across; the man seeking a more thorough appraisal of Monica's shoulder-length hair before being hauled back into the fray by his wife.

Three young men clad in thigh-tight jeans and *Hard-Rock* and *Jets* tee-shirts greeted her with winks, one pausing for any hint of a reaction, another taking a quick detour in the direction of a corner kiosk. A woman diverted her route to pass within viewing distance and quickly disappeared up the nearest flight of steps.

Monica held the book another half minute before returning it to its place on the stall.

She shuffled through a few successors eventually lifting *Virginia Queen* from the shelf. She examined the cover: a crown of thorns seeping onto the shoulder of a Confederate soldier's uniform. She turned, thrusting the book in the direction of the approaching traffic.

'*The Civil War...An isolated homestead in the midst of the battle front: A woman answers the door to find a close relative about to present her with the most heart-wrenching dilemma of her life.*'

She turned the book, watching a man stall by the shelf, waiting for his wife to catch up. Watching too as – on arrival – he leant his head and kissed her on the lips, the pair departing hand in hand.

It was as she was in the process of returning '*Virginia Queen*' to its place on the stand that a supposition of the last few minutes appeared to be confirmed: that she was being observed by someone standing a few yards beyond the far side of the shelves. On closer inspection it was a man; a short guy, maybe early thirties. A little dumpy and simple-looking like the ones you sometimes see being shepherded from place to place on a trip from one of those Day-Centres. Aware perhaps that he was himself coming under a degree of scrutiny, he took a few steps forwards.

'Books...!'

The announcement caught Monica only temporarily off-guard. She had been adjusting a few covers and was neither surprised nor unduly concerned to witness the man have everyone – mainly her – aware of his presence. She busied herself, shuffling a few more covers, knowing the way to deal with these guys was to make a show of ignoring them, whilst actually keeping them firmly in your sights, just in case. Initial impression was that he seemed fairly harmless, probably a bit nuts. You got them on the subway; it was like a magnet for them – the noise, constant movement, the general air of disorder. The thing was to press on regardless. She took another book from the rack, making a point of facing it toward the far end of the concourse.

'*Moving On.' A young girl – fresh from the suburbs, finds her life taking a new direction upon meeting an unlikely stranger...*'

The man had found his spot, like a day-tripper determined not to miss out on the slightest detail from the tour-guide. He shifted closer seeking a better handle on the woman's voice.

Monica took a few steps back, holding the book towards the barriers continuing to clatter the way to the downtown tracks. '*Seeks escape from the shackles of a world she has come to hate – and ultimately disown.*' The words were quickly lost in a hubbub of activity around a nearby cigarette kiosk.

The man stepped closer. It was like the guy up on the street waving the bibles, only she didn't shout so loud.

'How much?' he asked, striving to make himself heard above the melee both sides of the barrier. Monica stood her ground.

'Dollar-fifty.' The answer came as abruptly as the book was replaced on the shelf.

Stepping alongside, he lifted the book from its place, squinting at the title under the subdued light from the wall.

'I like books,' he said, making it come across like a public-announcement, further encouragement for Monica keeping her distance.

'I like books on cops,' he added, turning to the back-blurb before eyeing the shelf and its display of graphics and more visible titles.

'Asian Dream.' He read slowly, squinting into the title of the book sitting next to it, taking a moment to lift it from its place and skip through the pages. He looked up.

'Mc. Bain,' he said. 'I like Mc. Bain. You know Mc. Bain?'

Monica shook her head.

'87th Precinct. Cops! I like books on cops.'

The declaration drew him back to the shelf. As far as he could see there were no books on cops on the shelf, which wasn't to say there were no books on cops. Cops weren't always featured on the covers of books about cops.

'Drugs, rapes, murders, gang-fights...with Mc. Bain you get it all.'

Monica shuffled the titles, resolved to avoiding the guy's eye, the likelihood of him being nuts increasing by the second.

Moments later *Dynamite In Quilted Stockings* was raised to view. The man stepped back clearing the way for Monica to deliver the spiel.

'New England; a couple facing a new beginning and the kind of trauma that threatens to tear them apart...a new 'take' on the fragility lying at the heart of contemporary America.'

It brought some movement on the far side of the concourse. The man watched as a woman approached, casting an eye over the blurb and the cover's image of a wall-front with a stocking and a Stars & Stripes draped over it. A few exchanges followed as she reached for her purse. Monica took the money, depositing it in a belt concealed round her waist. Some way off the man's grin broadened.

'That's good,' he said. 'You sold one.'

The smile remained, encouraged at the sight of money exchanging hands as Monica adjusted the belt and continued to eye him a little more studiously, watching him fumble his way blindly across the spines. After brief hesitation, she picked a book from her end and handed it to him. Out of deference he took the book from her grasp.

'It's about a detective,' she said. 'Who forms a relationship with a serial-killer who's driven by a desire to see justice...on *her* terms.'

The man squinted at the cover.

'That's the sort of thing you get in Mc. Bain,' he said, turning the book a few times to gauge a little more of its content.

He held the book to the light for a few moments, not quite sure whether he was expected to hand it back or replace it on the shelf of his own volition.

Monica moved across, helping him make his decision. The man stood back, seeming relieved.

'With Mc. Bain you get it all: hookers, dope-fiends, gangs, gang-rapes...good cop-bad cop. It's all there,' he said.

He watched the book being replaced in its slot on the shelf. Once done, Monica looked across. The suggestion seemed to come from nowhere, and for no apparent reason – other than maybe an attempt to appease the guy a little.

'Okay – bring some.'

The man looked up startled, thinking maybe he was being admonished for interfering.

'Bring a few books and we'll share the float. You and me.' She seemed almost insistent. He looked up and down the concourse, checking whether anyone else was party to what was being suggested.

'Bring some books?' he asked, seeking confirmation he was hearing right and wasn't simply being chastised for interfering. Monica nodded.

'Yes, why not.' She shrugged and reached for the flask. 'Bring some and we can share the float – you and me!'

The man's face folded as he appeared to give the proposition a little thought.

'I'll have to ask Doreen,' he said. 'You think I should do that...ask Doreen?'

Monica could see no reason for not asking Doreen. She met the man's questioning look, a sharp contrast to the blank faces rushing to meet deadlines met only by catching the next downtown train.

'Yes. I think you should ask Doreen,' she said, returning to the shelf.

Resolved to not ignoring the advice, the man looked first one way and then the other. Turning to go, he paused, looking towards the nearest exit to the street.

'I think that will probably be okay.' The final call came from the foot of the steps.

'I'll ask Doreen,' he said.

Back at the shelf, Monica raised the next book to view. There was every reason to assume that would be the end of it. It wasn't unusual to get interruptions, but they rarely hung around long – like stray dogs or cats – and often more intrusive than *this* guy, even if he *was* a little nuts.

Which may well have been the case were it not for the sight, an hour or so later, of the same guy descending the steps clutching a plastic bag in his left hand. She watched his approach, not without some amusement, yet curious as to how events seemed likely to pan-out from here.

He had no hesitation in hoisting the bag to view.

'I saw Doreen. She said it was okay,' he said, waving the bag as confirmation and then placing it between his feet. 'Five books,' he confirmed. 'Cop books – Mc. Bain.'

And for the moment that would suffice. The books would remain in the bag. Only as, and when, instructed would he take any of the books from the bag.

'What's your name?' Monica asked, figuring she may as well get a handle on him rather than keep referring to him from a distance. Again, the man looked up like every question was a hefty kick aimed directly at the guts.

'Mac,' he called back. 'Everyone calls me that.'

'Okay Mac, pick your book,' she said, raising her voice to match his, watching as another wave of bodies descended the steps heading for the crescendo of noise beyond the line of barriers. Mac was down on his haunches. Choosing one would not be easy: homicides...rape...gang-rape...knifings...you got it all with Mc. Bain; most of it sitting right there at his feet. 'Your turn,' she said, with an exaggerated show of patience. Mac appeared to be in a state of some confusion.

'What do I do?' he asked, reduced to ditching the bag on the floor and spreading its contents like a deck of cards.

'Just pick a book, hold it on the air and say something about it – read from what it says on the back,' Monica explained, suddenly wary of coming across like one of those old-fashioned school-teachers.

Mac appeared less than convinced.

'Any book?' he asked, still fumbling and raising each cover in turn from the floor.

'Any book,' said Monica.

He finally drew himself to his feet, the book gripped tightly in one hand. Its cover was barely visible: an axe superimposed against a monochrome background. Monica was watching closely, seeing him take up a position under the mustard-yellow light – looking, for all the world, like a child about to perform in front of the class for the first time, the book raised in one hand.

'*Axe!*' The word belted out across the concourse; alarm-bells drawing people to a temporary halt.

'*There will be no happy new year for George Lasser...An axe has split his skull wide open...*' Mac completed the reading word for word from the blurb, each word as loud and as clear as the clicks of the barriers opposite.

Monica's turn. She stepped forward, *Kindle Fire* raised to view.

'California at the height of the Gold-Rush – a death in a family gives rise to a catalogue of feuds and divided loyalties: a tale of passion, fought against insurmountable odds.'

Seconds later Mac was finished fumbling around on the floor and back at his appointed spot, *Guns* gripped tightly in one hand.

'Colley Donato loved guns. He was sixteen when he first shot a guy. Brought up in Harlem, he lived amongst the hookers, pimps and junkies...'

He was beginning to get the hang of it; it was like the guy on 23rd Street waving the bibles and telling everyone they were going to die. Most people didn't listen to him either, but some did. Mirroring Monica he resumed his place on his corner, the book held high in one hand.

'Cops everywhere. Ex stripper Jeanine helped him, as did his friend Benny, a pimp from The Bronx.'

He looked along the shelf. 'It's like a game,' he said. 'You do a book – I do a book.'

Monica nodded. That was it *exactly*. The whole thing was a game – probably far more than he'd ever realise. She looked down, swapping two titles sitting side by side on the shelf.

The idea of people with deadlines to meet, mouths to feed, tv dinners to stick in the microwave, ball-games to take the kids to, climbing over each other or busting a gut to read about *'journeys of self-discovery'*...or *'new takes on the fragility at the heart of contemporary America'* was a delusion. These were ordinary people leading ordinary working lives. The same here in this city as in any other city. Which – odd as it may seem – was her sole reason for being down here. As Mac had aptly put it – it was simply her way of joining in the game...

It was pretty much on the stroke of eight-o-clock that Monica packed the last of the books away and raised the contraption to the wall. Mac watched, impressed at the way the frame hooked into place, the two placards slipping behind, out of sight, the stool cycle-locked by one of the ticket barriers. Watching too as Monica took the flask and popped it into a holdall she had kept at the side.

'Tomorrow,' he said, phrasing it like a question and looking across the gap between them.

Monica hooked the straps into place.

'Okay,' she said, drawing the holdall to her shoulder. 'Tomorrow.' Mac stood a moment longer occupying space that a few hours earlier had been a constant hub of activity. 'Okay...' he said. 'Tomorrow.'

She watched him take the plastic bag in one hand and make his way to the steps at the far end of the concourse before turning to make a move in the opposite direction.

The following day began the same as any other – Monica striding briskly along the sidewalk, stepping gingerly down the steps, bobbing and weaving to avoid the entourage of early-morning traffic, finally reaching her familiar spot next to the poster for the city's Philharmonic & Jazz Ensemble.

It was as she was grounding the case that she spotted the notice. It was a flyer, the kind you got all over the city, evidently pinned there before the rest of the city had stirred. She was the only one who appeared to have noticed it or be paying it any attention. The message was simple enough, pinned to a spot where the shelf would be attached to the wall...

Order of the City Authority.
Area to be kept clear.
Commercial activity restricted to licence-holders only.
Dated...Signed...

The lower quarter was stamped with the Metropolitan insignia and signed in two places: a city police stamp and reference-number included in the lower corner.

Monica re-read the notice and on a third reading, grounded the case and reached to unlock the top catches. The shelf could remain where it was for now but the placards needed to be removed, and some of the books. She stood a moment against the wall.

It seemed even colder standing there without the shelf to keep her company. The only thing that remained was the flask of coffee. She undid the top and poured some of the contents into the lid. It was as on previous days, tepid and unappetising. It was as she was refilling the cup that she was aware of someone standing at her side staring up at the notice.

Plastic bag clutched in one hand, Mac was staring hard at the words pinned to the wall. With the lady sitting there drinking coffee and no sign of the books, he had got the gist of the message. He grounded the plastic-bag and looked back and forth across the concourse, squinting first at the people headed for the barriers, and then at Monica crouched on her haunches nursing the plastic cup in both hands.

Then he looked again at the notice, the contents of his bag forgotten for a moment.

'They stopped it.' Monica continued to sip the coffee, her eye following the hustle and bustle of activity in and around the barriers opposite. Mac re-examined the notice on the off-chance he had missed anything.

'Why they do that?'

Monica finished the coffee and replaced the lid on the flask. No-one – certainly not Monica – seemed able to come up with an answer.

'They shouldn't have done that,' Mac insisted, reaching for his bag, unsure now what would happen, having brought his books: the same five books from yesterday.

'Doreen said it was okay,' he said, raising the bag by way of illustration and staring hard in both directions.

Monica brushed her hands and rose to her feet. She reached for the case and unclasped the lid.

He watched her take some of the books from the shelf and pack them in the limited space in the case, then reach to pull the scarf tight and finally lean down to take hold of the case. There would be the removal of the frame and bolts to consider. But that could come later. She lifted the case from the ground.

Mac had one eye on the notice, the other on his next move, something he hadn't bargained on; maybe get to Coney Island, watch the guys selling hot-dogs on the sea-front or back to 23rd street watching the guy waving the bibles.

Monica snapped the case shut and was pulling the scarf more tightly round her neck.

'I don't know why they stopped it,' she said, pulling the hat firmly on her head and looking at Mac.

At the sound of her voice, Mac turned.

Seconds later Monica was to be seen bobbing and weaving her way in and out of the steady movement of people on her way to the exit.

'I like books on cops,' Mac announced, still rooted to the spot and speaking now to anyone in the vicinity who might be prepared to listen, before reaching for the plastic bag at his feet.

⤙⤚

Some lines quoted from the blurb of 'Guns' by Ed McBain... Pan books Ltd. London SW10 9PG

Four Men In A Boat

It was the dead of night on the fringe of the ocean. Four figures – at first glance, as alike as four peas in a pod – sat huddled in seats, their features struggling for recognition above the splutter of the boat's engine and the steady sweep of the ocean ahead.

'Bit choppy then,' said Harold, taking a firm grip on the starboard side.

'Bit,' said Maurice, following his example on the opposite side.

'Dark too,' said Tom, following their eyes to the farthest reaches of the ocean.

'Dark enough,' agreed Harold. 'Save for the moon.'

At the first pull of the engine voices dropped and all eyes turned. Somewhere out there a different voice beckoned, a familiar voice perhaps – yet one about to set them adrift from tiny coves of shingle and out onto the open sea.

'Okay boatswain?' came the call from the rear. There would be little response from the front of the boat, the boatswain having an eye only on the line that would take them clear of the final thrust of the promontory.

And in due time the others would follow, each taking the opportunity to breathe the night air and eye a phantom-like line of cliffs bidding their own silent goodbyes to the four figures huddled together drifting out onto the open sea beneath them.

'Beautiful,' said Maurice.

With the bags stowed out of harm's way, it was down to Harold – breathing a little more easily with terra-firma finally behind them – to turn to the others.

'So Tom, how goes it with you on this wild moonlit night?'

'Oh not so bad, not so bad.' There was an expectant hush in the air, evident on both sides of the boat.

'Can't complain,' he said.

'And Joe.' Harold looked up, catching Joe's eye. 'How does the world find Joe this evening?'

'Oh as they go,' said Joe, slotting into his customary mode of responding with an air of one who had little to say on the matter.

'And boatswain! How about you?' Again it was Harold's voice reaching out – on this occasion directed solely to the front of the boat. 'Going to give us a shanty of two to keep us entertained on our nocturnal hike across the ocean?'

'No not me...' said the boatswain, his eye as steady as his voice in maintaining a line that would hopefully steer them beyond the last throes of land without undue interruption.

It was with time to kill and all eyes on a tiny block of land waiting patiently in the far reaches of the ocean that the closing of ranks began...

It would be down to Harold to get proceedings underway. He stretched his legs and looked to his right.

'So Tom – the garden. Tell us your plans for the garden...'

Bodies reclined in time with the gentle rhythm of the boat as Tom collected his thoughts and steadied himself to begin.

'The garden,' he began. 'Okay...Well, what I'm thinking is...keep everything low-key; the whole right hand side from the gate upwards – trellis fencing; flag-stone paving fanning out from the path to a sealing-stone patio reaching as far as the rear door.'

There were murmurs on both sides.

'Sounds good to me Tom. What do you think Mo?'

'Sounds good to me,' said Maurice.

'And...' said Harold, looking to press on and nodding for Tom to take it from there. Tom inhaled deeply, taking his own private tour of the scene before sharing it with the others.

'Lower half of the garden: tiny rockery, small whirlpool, stream meandering down over the rocks, down through a channel cut out as far as the end of the garden, down the crags and off into the open sea!'

'Beautiful,' said Harold. 'What do you think Mo? Tiny stream running down the crags and off into the open sea?'

'Sounds good,' said Mo.

'Beautiful,' said Joe.

'And…' said Harold, arms stretched along both sides of the boat. 'Fill us in on the rest Tom.'

'Well… like we said, trellis fence, tarred, weather-proofed, reaching the patio area just beneath the window, similarly tiled – barbecue basin, brick surround_'

'And….'

'Plastic hood, retractable when, or if, it rains,' said Tom, completing the picture with an emphatic slap on the side of the boat.

'Alfresco-eating for the summer months,' breathed Harold, turning his eye to the front of the boat.

'What do you say Boatswain? You going to come and christen the barbecue with us – nice bit of belly-pork, bit of salad – fresh grown in the garden?'

'No not me,' said the boatswain, his eye fixed on keeping a firm grip on the throttle ahead of a wave of turbulence set to disturb them over the next few metres. 'Not on this occasion.' Harold chuckled and extended a second arm along the rear of the boat.

'Not a pork man,' he said, turning to the others with a grin.

There was a murmur of assent, each taking a moment to observe the swells beginning to broaden alongside them like the backs of giant whales – a sure sign they were beyond the shores of one home, whilst drawing ever closer to another….

Again, it would be down to Harold – eyes closed, thoughts drifting to within the four walls – to take things from there.

'So…Joe – the kitchen. Tell us your plans for the kitchen.'

It was Joe's turn to grip the boat's side, tapping each idea in time with the rise and fall of the surrounding ocean.

'Well when it comes to the kitchen, it's a question of utilising space to maximum efficiency.'

'That's right,' said Harold. 'You with us there Mo?'

'Absolutely,' said Mo... 'Maximum use of space equals maximum efficiency.'

'That's right,' said Joe. 'So...'

An arm extended, taking them the first few feet inside the timber-frame door. 'Stainless-steel splash-back, quarry tiles. Corian worktops. Roof lights guaranteeing maximum use of available space.'

'Excellent,' said Harold, quick to show his approval, allowing Joe a moment before completing the picture. 'And...'

'Multi-fuel stove allowing tightly-controlled temperatures to reach as far as the hallway – and beyond.'

'That's it,' said Harold.

'Temperatures rarely fluctuating beyond fifteen, sixteen degrees – depending on the degree of external sunlight.'

'Absolutely,' said Maurice. 'Minimum sun – maximum control.'

'Maximum sun – minimum control,' said Tom.

Harold looked approvingly, tapping the boat's side and casting a casual nod to the front of the vessel.

'What about you boatswain. You going to join us for a fillet-steak – medium rare, cooked over a multi-fuel stove – bit of salad from the garden – bowl of shellfish soup fresh from the rockery?'

The boatswain's eye had switched to a line of lights traversing the scene some several miles in the distance.

'No – not me,' he said. 'Not on this occasion.'

Harold chuckled. 'Not a meat man,' he said, looking across at the others.

There was a moment's reprieve: chance for Mo to reach down and take a small packet from the haversack at his side. All eyes were on him as he withdrew a small cellophane packet and began unravelling its contents.

'Corned beef,' he said, looking to inspect the roll for confirmation. The moment passed – chance for Mo to make in-roads into the packet's contents. And join the others observing clusters of stars arched like stacks of diamonds across the black expanse of sky.

It was after a minute or so's contemplation that Harold was back to spreading his arms along either side of the boat.

'So, Mo – the bathroom,' he began. 'Lets hear your plans for the bathroom.'

'Okay,' said Maurice, shuffling into place and closing his eyes to picture the scene.

'What I'm thinking is: all four walls…porcelain tiles, probably ivory – neutral colour.' A hand stretched to indicate the extent of the décor in mind. 'Light-drops, port-hole window – effective, yet without compromising on privacy.'

There were nods on both sides.

'Privacy's key in the bathroom,' said Tom.

'And the bath Mo…' said Harold. 'Tell us what plans you've got for that.'

Again Maurice took a moment to dwell on what would be one of his all-time favourite features.

'Free-standing, possibly off-white or butter-cream; single-spout…sixty, sixty-five degree angled surround.'

'And…' said Harold.

'Chrome handles – ceramic brown tiles but with timber-base bordering two to three feet within available wall-space.'

'What do you reckon Tom?'

'Fit for a queen,' said Tom.

'Or king,' said Maurice.

'What about you boatswain?' The cry was levelled to where the boatswain had reset his sights on a more distant chain of lights – likely a container-vessel wending its way into the far-off waters. 'Fancy lying in a bath of bubbles against a sixty to sixty-five degree angled surround?'

'No not me,' came the reply. 'Not on this occasion.'

Harold chuckled. 'Not one for lying back in a sea of bubbles,' he said with a grin. 'You catch that Joe, Mo…Not one for lying in a sea of bubbles, the boatswain!'

'Not him,' said Joe.

'Not a bubbles man,' said Maurice with a grin.

The men fell silent.

There would, in due course, be more to come – sufficient to keep them busy for a good while yet: ground-source heat pumps from Joe, the ins-and-outs of fibre-cementing, drainage-channels and the viability of solar-panelling: all possibilities waiting to slot into place with the tiny block of land drawing ever-closer.

The boatswain too was finally able to settle; the sea reduced to a few gentle undulations as the jagged line of land drew into view.

All eyes turned on its clearly defined line of rocks, even more prominent under the illumination of moonlight.

It was down to the boatswain to negotiate the final approach: a quick throw of the throttle-control to engage the clutch and the final throw into reverse.

The final task – the hauling of a rope around what appeared to be a metal stanchion to the side of a small jetty.

Above them a line of crags stretched to one side and somewhere amongst them, a path that would take them above the rocks to their agreed rendezvous point.

One by one, taking each other by the arm, the four men stepped from the boat close to the jut of land that – even at this angle – bore close resemblance to the snout of a giant crocodile.

Behind them the boatswain would complete his formalities for the night – securing the vessel to its mooring point and reckoning up the fuel against the amount indicated on the dial. Having done that, he turned to pocket the notes handed over by Harold.

'Same time next month,' said Harold.

The boatswain nodded and drew the steps back into the pit of the boat. Behind him, the men began the ascent to the path that would return them to the terra-firma of a few hours previous; Harold leading the way, the others huddled behind him: to a man looking very much the business in their waist-length rubber leggings and thigh-length rubber boots.

It was at the top of the cliff looking back across the familiar bank of ocean that the men stopped, the ritual hand-shaking completing their evening.

'Same time next month then Maurice…?'

'Yep…next month.'

'You too Joe?'

'Count me in,' said Joe.

All four turned to the road, Harold leading them to where the car was waiting some four hundred yards away. It would be a short drive to the pub.

'Your round I believe,' said Harold, looking across the car at Joe.

'That's right,' said Joe, checking to make sure his wallet hadn't dropped out of his pocket clambering from the boat.

'Definitely your round,' said Maurice.

The Go-Between

As M.J. Meredith strolled to where a gravel drive narrowed to a typically ornate floral heart-shaped display, he had little on his mind beyond a determination to create the right impression, to ensure that he didn't say, or do, anything untoward. Yet looking round and judging from the general state of the place, he was beginning to wonder just what sort of an impression might be considered favourable – the word 'opulence' hardly one to spring to mind. Scanning his eye along one side and even the front of the house there was nothing particularly *opulent*, or grand about the place at all: the whole of one side and the bit visible from round the back little more than a jungle of weeds amidst piles of junk and discarded furniture.

Feeling some relief at venturing into more humble surroundings than he'd envisaged, he reached for a brass bell-button fixed into the wall and took a step back to take in the pebble-dashed façade and to make another quick check on his watch. For all the shabbiness there was something about these places made you particularly sensitive about arriving too early or too late.

There was a moment's delay before the door opened and a tiny woman who Meredith thought looked rather like a little Dutch doll with pixie eyes stood aside to admit him to the lobby. No words were exchanged as he was led along a hall lined with antique paintings to another door where the pair stopped and the woman brushed herself down, knocked and waited.

Like the rear and side of the house, there was a shambolic feel about the room into which he was admitted. Loose pillows and bits of bric-a-brac lay scattered around; a few items of discarded clothing and a huge black hole of a fireplace opposite. Faded curtains and a dining table scuffed at the edges dominated one side of the room. Floral décor sofa and arm-chairs occupied most of the remaining space.

In a corner, seated in a huge Edwardian arm-chair deliberately placed facing the window, a figure sat wrapped in a shawl, resolved it seemed to paying little heed to whatever commotion had seen fit to disturb her afternoon. Only when such time had lapsed that it might become a little too embarrassing for everyone, did she make a three-quarter turn to greeting him.

The face that met him was a rather drab face, a little elongated with eyes of a tiny sparrow and a mouth that was little more than a tiny slit between her cheekbones. When she spoke, her voice was flat, virtually devoid of intonation.

'You'll be Mr. Meredith,' the announcement struggling to make it through the miniscule aperture of her mouth.

Meredith acknowledged the point. Having confirmed his identity she levelled an arm at the chair opposite.

'Take a seat Mr. Meredith.'

Having allowed him time to compose himself: arms folded in business-like fashion across his knees, she finally arranged herself to award him her full attention. Even at this juncture there was a timidity, almost a frailty about her, as if the whole business of communication was an ordeal best avoided – a consequence perhaps of a life spent gazing at four blank walls and a ramshackle garden, and maybe explaining a tendency to repeatedly seek distraction in whatever caught her eye at the foot of the garden. She blinked and seemed to stutter over the words, before settling herself sufficiently to get to the point.

'Mr. Meredith. The facts are simple.' She spoke simply and effortlessly, pulling on each finger in turn and for the first time looking him directly in the eye. 'The facts are – I can neither read nor write.'

Her grip on the fingers tightened at the disclosure, beyond which, she appeared to have little to say.

Meredith acknowledged the fact with a curt nod. The advert in the County magazine had hinted along such lines, if only vaguely. Relieved at detecting little beyond casual acknowledgement, she shifted herself to a more business-like posture and reached for the bell that – in a matter of minutes – would bring a delivery of a tray of afternoon tea and cake, delivered by the tiny shuffling woman with the pixie eyes.

On its arrival Meredith waited for the ritual pouring and stirring, finally taking his cup and saucer from the tray and sipping politely at its contents, taking care not to let the tiny handle slip in his cumbersome grasp.

The woman took her cup and placing it delicately on the saucer, introduced herself as Hyacinth Maybury.

'You'll likely be amused at the name,' she said, sipping sedately and almost managing a smile. Meredith returned the smile, though again only out of politeness. He'd heard far stranger names. If anything there was something rather quaint about it, something endearingly 'English'. Seeming relieved for the second time in quick succession, she replaced the cup on the saucer.

'I don't mind,' she said, seeming suddenly disposed to talking about these things quite openly.

'My mother loved flowers – particularly hyacinths.' Again, a trace of a smile threatened to break across the tiny carp-like mouth.

And again Meredith returned the smile.

Though hardly an earth-shattering start to proceedings, he appeared to have avoided any major rucks and a number of possibilities had already sprung to mind regarding the woman's circumstances: a divorcee possibly, husband likely moved on, or maybe even deceased – there was definitely a melancholic feel about the whole place. Or maybe a spinster, if such terms still existed. Certainly, you got the feeling there was a tale to tell were one to probe a little deeper.

'My mother's dead,' she said, as if reading his thoughts and lowering cup and saucer to her lap.

Meredith waited for anything of further significance to arise from the disclosure.

There was little beyond a sigh and a further twisting of fingers. It was some moments later that they returned to more immediate matters.

'Mr. Meredith, as I can neither read nor write your duties are simple, and not at all excessively time-consuming.'

She continued to view him through sharp squinting eyes.

'Mr. Meredith, your task is to write letters on my behalf, and…' She coughed nervously and looked to her lap. 'And to read the replies…'

There was again no visible reaction. He'd imagined his duties *would* be fairly modest. What else should one expect of a private secretarial post in the heart of the Oxfordshire countryside?

It was after placing cup and saucer on the table that Hyacinth braced herself for what was arguably the only revelation to emerge thus far…

'Mr. Meredith – the letters are to my lover…'

There was again little reaction from the seat opposite. Given his duties were to be secretarial, it was always likely to involve letters. To whom they were directed was neither here nor there: lawyers…lovers, it was all one and the same to him; if each paid as handsomely as the other what was there to choose between them?

He reached for his cup. At the end of the day, her opening observation had been the most telling one: that his duties seemed unlikely to prove excessively demanding.

Again relieved at the lack of any visible reaction, she raised the plate to resume a moment's refreshment.

For all the ease of the exchanges it did seem a rather bizarre arrangement: a woman living alone, for whatever reason illiterate, given to corresponding with a lover…wherever/ whoever he may be; her only apparent company – a tiny woman with pixie eyes who shuffled in and out bearing pots of tea. An obvious question, and one that hadn't escaped him – why *she* wouldn't be better disposed to dealing with Her Ladyship's correspondence? Unless, of course, she too was ill-equipped to fulfil the task. It was all a little peculiar and already begged the question...was he being invited to read more between the lines than might be about to appear on the page?

But for now at least, it would remain mere conjecture; more pressing matters awaited.

'Now, Mr. Meredith, you'll take a pen and paper – both are in the desk at the side there.

He would indeed do just that. He rose and opened the lid – a fine old oakwood veneer. She watched – observing him retrieve pen and paper from the drawer and sit with both comfortably placed on his knee.

'You do shorthand Mr. Meredith. It was clarified in your letter I believe.'

Meredith closed the lid and confirmed this was so, a prerequisite for having been offered the job back in town.

'Good.'

Hyacinth positioned herself a little more convivially on the edge of her seat – a position ideally suited to getting one's thoughts into some sort of perspective. A moment too for him to practise a few quick manoeuvres with the wonderful fine-nibbed pen.

She coughed, resuming the clenching of fingers in her lap.

'It's a letter Mr. Meredith, you understand.'

Having presumed as much, he nodded.

There was a moment's hesitation – the opening paragraph to one's lover not one to scupper through undue haste; plus, no doubt, a moment to reflect at having one's emotional baggage unavoidably thrust into the public domain...

My dearest love...

Meredith watched her attention flit to the far end of the garden.

It has been a while since pen has been put to paper, but – you'll understand there being just cause for the delay.

Again she paused, prepared to devote what time was required to finding the appropriate words:

Darling, you must know, as I sit here in a state of semi-solitude, that the only words that matter...

She looked back, catching a glimpse of Meredith's pen gliding effortlessly across the page...*are that I love you dearly! more than simple words can ever come close to expressing: more than a lion loves its cubs or a mother loves her new-born child. And the times we are apart are times I think only of being mauled by wild beasts or subjected to abominable medieval tortures...'*

There was a moment to draw breath and for Meredith to take the opportunity to check the shorthand annotation of this – his first piece of work for quite a while.

'What do you think?' She glanced across, apparently looking to Meredith to offer some kind of meaningful appraisal.

Mindful of his resolve back on the gravel drive, he thought about it a moment and nodded. 'Makes its point,' he said.

'There's more.' Hyacinth was quickly back to her former pose, again appearing to draw inspiration from the scene beyond the window.

My dearest love. When I'm awake I think only of you, and when I'm asleep I dream only of you. And as I lie in my bed I see only you, and feel only you – pulling me tight – in arms that would surely never let me go...these are moments when I become your rag-doll, and you, my love, become the puppet-master...

Again she turned to see Meredith's pen skipping lightly across the paper.

'Okay?'

Meredith nodded. Quite what she expected him to say he couldn't be sure – if anything, or whether it would likely swing proceedings one way or the other. *If* she wanted a genuine opinion, that it seemed little more than a load of self-indulgent twaddle, he could of course oblige; though already he had the impression of something else going on here – a voice wrestling with issues that went beyond a few limp pleas for approval.

'You obviously like him a lot,' he managed to blurt out. Either it failed to register or it was a gross understatement.

Hyacinth leant closer, the carp-like mouth nibbling anxiously at her lower lip.

'Mr. Meredith,' she said, her voice dropping an octave. 'I adore the man. She looked hard at Meredith, her arms folded neatly across her tiny bosom. 'Do you understand what I'm saying?' Meredith nodded, and on this occasion made a point of not smiling.

She bowed her head, hands clasped to her heart.

'Another line Mr. Meredith – if you will!' There was a hint of irritation, as much in the line as in the voice behind it.

And darling, time without you is time wasted; Pray God I continue to feel your hot breath burning into my neck, if only from a distance. I remain your devoted lover...forever... H x...

It was a predictably curt conclusion and all that remained was for Meredith to seat himself at the desk a few feet away to get the thing into a form of prose, to be read back to her some ten minutes later – allowing her opportunity to sip tea and gaze wistfully towards the lower reaches of the garden.

It appeared to tick all the boxes; Meredith watched hands clasped approvingly as she indicated a stack of envelopes in the chest of drawers from which he had taken pen and paper.

Having put their first afternoon's work behind them, there was opportunity to relax; to lean back, inviting Meredith to share a moment's reflection.

'Ah...Mr. Meredith, if only you'd met my Jacob. What a man...! Charismatic, charming, and...' She looked toward late afternoon already beginning to gather at the foot of the garden. 'A wonderful lover.' Her eyelids fluttered for a moment, her gaze dropping to her lap. 'You know what I mean by that Mr. Meredith.'

For once Meredith fought to suppress a smile.

It was as he was about to pop the lid back on the pen that she stalled a moment, leaning inquisitively, fingers tapping lightly against the chair arm.

'Tell me Mr. Meredith...are you a travelling man?' As unexpected as an unlikely question coming as it did from one who appeared to spend her time glued to a chair in the midst of the Oxfordshire countryside. And did she mean 'Traveller' as in Romany or a frequenter of foreign parts?

'Traveller,' she repeated, taking a lack of response as a sign that maybe she hadn't made herself clear. 'A frequenter of foreign parts: Paris...Rome...Venice...Vienna? The great cities of the world.'

Meredith shrugged.

'Not really,' he said, which – given the circumstances – seemed to him an expedient enough answer.

Hmm...that's interesting,' she said, setting the cup on the saucer and staring into murky ripples of tea.

'To travel. To see the world. Wonderful places – wonderful people...of all creeds, of all colours?' She reached across, putting the cup to one side; the world and its numerous attractions appearing to go on hold for a moment.

Meredith finished popping the pen-lid, waiting to see what, in any, further demands were to be made of his time. Very little it seemed.

'So...we'll leave it there for today – our first day. I thank you for your services. My maid will see you out. She'll also take the letter which will be addressed, stamped and posted post-haste to my lover, and place an envelope in your hand at the door, in which you'll find the details of your next appointment.'

She looked to confirm Meredith was in agreement, or whether – on reflection – he was having second thoughts about his new-found employment.

'Is that okay with you Mr. Meredith?'

'Yes – that's fine,' said Meredith, shaking himself to his feet and unsure whether his departure was to be accompanied by the shaking of hands. The fee, negotiated by prior arrangement, was a generous one and would be placed in his hand at the conclusion of each session.

No sooner had the pixie-woman seen him out of the door than Meredith took the opportunity to shake the formality of the last half hour or so from his limbs and consider his next move – namely, getting himself back to town. A brisk walk seemed favourite, followed by a few pints in one of the taverns he'd spotted in the High Street, the middle tavern, *The Horse's Mouth* appearing, at first glance, a distinct possibility.

Once back in town and having found the tavern stocked with a reasonable selection of ales he took his place at a table in the corner. Beer and dry-roasted peanuts – the ideal foundation for reflecting on his afternoon's work and particularly the fee that accompanied it, which – on further clarification handed to him by the pixie-woman – was to be no mean sum. Plus, the equally valid observation that there were far more strenuous ways of earning it. That the woman was likely nuts, or as close to it as warranted description, was neither here nor there. If anything – it was a plus: nutty people being more prone to such flights-of-fancy than the certifiably sane. If all that was required was to get it all down on paper, then who was he to let the opportunity pass?

All in all, a promising afternoon's work, deserving one more in this pub before moving on to the next: a pint of 'Old' this time: a darker ale and a bit stronger at over five-per-cent, but nothing less than he deserved after an afternoon at the service of Hyacinth Maybury.

It was at the appointed time on the appointed date that Meredith next rang the bell and took a few steps back, waiting for the pixie-woman to admit him to the living room where he encountered Hyacinth Maybury in a familiar pose – seated, feet folded, on the same chair, her attention directed to the foot of the garden.

The procedure was equally familiar: a moment's delay before acknowledging the disturbance behind her.

'Mr. Meredith.' She turned with a half smile and prepared herself in her chair.

Meredith nodded and awaited the invitation to take the weight off his feet.

'Take a seat Mr. Meredith.' She extended an arm at the same chair of a few days ago. Taking up the invitation he pondered the likelihood of there being a time when they might dispense with the formalities of surnames. Smiling – this time entirely to himself – he positioned himself to begin, noting that Hyacinth appeared to be in a singularly upbeat mood.

'So, Mr. Meredith,' she said again, almost managing to force to smile. 'Lovely day.' She broke her pose to direct her attention to a shaft of sunlight breaking above the pile of discarded furniture at the foot of the garden and to reach for the bell at her side. Seconds later, the pixie-woman put in her second appearance of the day, and minutes later, a third, as she placed tea-pot and plate of biscuits on the table at their sides.

Overriding any need for an invitation, Meredith reached across for a biscuit, watching the pixie-woman retrace her steps and promptly disappear from the scene.

His thoughts were interrupted as Hyacinth abandoned the view beyond the house to lean across, an expression of curiosity resurfacing as on his previous visit.

'Tell me Mr. Meredith...are you a sporting man? Tennis? Squash?...Badminton?'

Meredith gave an impression of giving it a little thought before responding with a now customary shrug.

'Not really,' he said, which was pretty close to the truth, unless trotting down the road to one's local pub four times a week counted as 'sporting'.

'Hmm, that's interesting,' she said, drawing the sleeves of her blouse together and clasping one hand firmly over the other.

'And the arts? Are you artistically inclined?....Fine painting..?' She extended a hand in the direction of the hallway. 'The theatre...cinema...fine literature...good music?'

Again he did the polite thing of hesitating briefly so as not to appear too emphatic about it.

'Not really.'

Tipping a half teaspoon of sugar into her cup she sought to pursue it a little.

'Good music?...Mozart...Debussy?'

'Not as a rule,' he said, following her example of stirring the contents of his cup and content enough to have the bill for his services mount before even thinking of getting down to business.

'Mm...That's interesting,' she said, her expression lengthening, her voice wavering a fraction.

'You'll take a letter,' she said.

Back in the pub, pint of 'Old' and a packet of nuts at the ready, he drew his calculator from his pocket. A few taps on the keyboard were quick to confirm it: hour for hour, given the minimum daily rate confirmed both verbally and in writing, it was unquestionably the easiest money he'd earned in his life. Having established the now-likely routine he could afford to be even more thorough in his calculations, concluding that at little more than thirty minutes per session, at a pay-rate stipulated in the advert and guaranteed by the agency in town, even allowing for a few pints before catching his train – he'd be quids in. Easy meat – easy money! He raised his glass, downing a good third of its contents with an appreciative smack of his lips. As to the pixie-woman; quite how she fitted into the picture was anybody's guess. Presumably she had to do something to earn her crust.

It was at the start of session three that the envelope was handed to him the minute he'd taken his seat, whilst Hyacinth, clad in ankle-length smock, her hair tied to a bun speared by what appeared to be a long wooden skewer, sat back observing him from the seat opposite.

'Mr. Meredith; a favour if you will.'

He had been immediately taken-aback to see her indicate a long envelope, inviting him to reach up and investigate its contents.

'It is from my lover – from Jacob,' she announced, sitting suddenly straight-backed in her chair.

'Mr. Meredith, I've been in possession of the letter for three days now. Three days of seeing it sitting there in its little box – so close and yet so agonisingly far. Can you imagine what that means to a poor illiterate soul such as you see before you Mr. Meredith?'

Meredith took the envelope and turned it a few times.

The watermark appeared to be authentic – an official Devonshire Post Office watermark stuck there next to the stamp and address.

'Well?' said Hyacinth, virtually beside herself and near enough pulling each finger from its socket.

Meredith swallowed hard as he tore the white foolscap apart and reached inside.

First thing was an address – all there, neatly printed in the top right corner; and then, next to it, a date – the whole thing, including the lines beneath, in perfectly presented type-written print.

But it was what followed that instantly touched a far more sensitive nerve, causing him to cough and give an impression of turning the opening words over in his mind, if for no other reason...a reminder of the need to buy the pair of them a little more time.

For all the simplicity of the words it was far from an easy read____

Dear H. This will not be easy. In fact it will be difficult. I thank you for your kind words. But – there is little to be gained from beating about the bush. As you say, the distance between us is huge – like the distance between Saturn and Pluto, which got me thinking. And what I've thought is that though I 'like' you, I don't 'love' you. And – as a result – I don't

*want to go out with you any more and think it best if we called
it a day.*

> *Sorry H...but I'm sure you'll find someone else; someone
> who understands you, and treats you right. But...the
> fact is – I can't be that person.*
> *Hope you're well; regards!*
> *J*
> X
> *PS: I haven't found anyone else, just in case you were
> wondering.*

Meredith read it a third time, his brain already working
feverishly. Aside from Hyacinth Maybury's world about to hit
the buffers, his own future was suddenly looking decidedly
dodgy. With the elusive Jacob about to disappear from the
scene there was every reason to assume he might be following
suit.

The voice from the seat opposite was anything but patient.

'Mr. Meredith...please!'

He rustled the paper, managing a casual nod.

'Yes – he's doing good; says he's fine...'

'And...Mr. Meredith...please...!'

Meredith swallowed, turning the sheet a couple of times.

'Says he respects you and_____'

'Mr. Meredith, *read* the words. I must hear the words
spoken plainly, as if *you* were Jacob; so it is *his* words speaking
directly to me. Do you understand Mr. Meredith?' The tiny
eyes were suddenly ablaze. 'Don't you see – I want *you* to be
my Jacob. Surely you see that is the whole point...'

Meredith readied himself, a professional's instinct just
about able to assume control. He thought quickly...

Darling...he began, skimming the page as convincingly
as circumstances permitted...*lovely to hear from you. I'm
fine and like you say – our love is strong – I see and feel its*

strength on a daily basis, the miles between us neither here nor there.

'Oh Mr. Meredith – please...read on.'

Meredith read on...A few 'darlings', a few kisses, a line about vice-like arms never letting one another go...And finally____

Love U lots
J XXX

Hyacinth clapped her hands and reached for a slice of cake.

'Ah...Mr. Meredith. Words, words, words...where would we be without them?

She tipped her cup to empty the remainder of its contents.

'You'll take a slice of cake Mr. Meredith. And then – a letter.'

He reached across more than happy to oblige on both counts.

It was over a pint and a packet of nuts that the Plan-B began to take shape. The point being, as he would repeatedly remind himself – to all intents and purposes, little had changed, or – more importantly – needed to change: Her Ladyship still shut away in her chamber, and to the best of her knowledge young Jacob still typing away merrily somewhere in the wilds of Devon. All that was required was to keep the thing moving calmly and swiftly between them, without the need for either to shift from their seats or to be calling anything into question – the content of the letters suddenly neither here nor there.

Thankfully he'd had the foresight to think ahead a little back in the house, suggesting saving Her Ladyship and her maid the time and trouble of plodding off to the nearest post-box, when he was heading for town himself and could easily pop the letter in the box for her. Her eyes had widened with delight at the suggestion.

'Mr.Meredith, you'd really do that – for me?'

Meredith had been quick to reassure her it would be absolutely no problem.

It was over his second pint that the pieces began to slot more firmly into place: that though a letter, of sorts, needed to arrive from Jacob – ie. from Devon, the only requirement was evidence of it having actually *come* from Devon: a watermark, but – and this was key – the same one as before; for you could bet your bottom dollar the pixie-woman would be over the envelope like flies on a cowpat the minute it dropped through the letter-box.

The solution – go to Devon and post the letter himself! He'd done the maths: he was being paid handsomely enough. A round-trip to Devon would hardly eat into his earning as to make it untenable. A day's work, a change of air for a few hours, the cost of a return fare; he'd still be quids in!

And – no need for any more of these dumb letters; just a few typewritten scribbles on a piece of paper, stick it in an envelope, jump on a train, quick dash across the moor courtesy of the local bus to the appropriate post-office – he'd be back in his digs before nightfall.

It was three days into the following week, having put phase-one of his plan successfully behind him, that he made his way up the drive and reached for the brass button for the pixie-woman to escort him to putting phase-two into operation. Seconds later he was in her Lady's boudoir, and seconds after that – ushered to his seat.

'Mr. Meredith.' She turned in her customary convivial manner to face him.

'Inside the box Mr. Meredith...' She wasted no time in having Meredith reach across and take the envelope from the small trinket-box on the table.

'From Jacob – my lover!' she announced, hands clasped once more across her tiny chest.

'Mr. Meredith. What does my loved-one say? For two days the thing has been sitting there – the suspense more than a poor illiterate woman such as you see before you can bear. Pray get yourself into position to become my Jacob. Let me see *him* as I see *you* – sharing my afternoon over slices of lemon cake and fresh tea.'

She looked with beseeching eyes as Meredith calmly reached for the envelope and with a quick flick of the finger tore the flap open.

Following the tribulations of the previous visit, it would be hopefully be plain sailing from hereon. He flicked the page, making a point of checking each carefully crafted line.

'Oh…Mr. Meredith,' she announced, putting the cup to one side on completion of the reading. 'Words, words, words. My Jacob has such a way with words. Don't you agree?' Meredith nodded. Certainly he had a way with words. Only a fool would deny it.

Hyacinth refilled her cup and extended a plate of lemon-drizzle slices in his direction. 'Ahh…Mr. Meredith. If only you could meet the man.'

For a moment she appeared to hesitate – as if suddenly recalling some issue she'd hitherto overlooked.

'And yet – I do hope this doesn't sound *entirely* stupid…But I almost feel you *are* Jacob, sitting here, drinking tea and eating cake. Does that sound entirely ridiculous Mr. Meredith?'

Meredith took a bite of cake. All things considered – nothing that occurred in the household of Hyacinth Maybury could count as entirely ridiculous.

'Now – you'll take a letter.'

'Ah Mr. Meredith,' came the familiar voice from the armchair on the afternoon of the third day of the following week. 'Take a seat please.'

'You are well Mr. Meredith.' Meredith nodded, increasingly at ease in his re-defined role as he sat waiting for her to reach for the bell to have the pixie-woman appear brandishing tea, biscuits or whatever other delights might be seen as fitting accompaniment to Jacob's most recent communication.

'Ah…Mr. Meredith. yet again I have heard from my beloved.' Again there was an edge to the voice rather in the manner of a child admitting to currying favour with a teacher.

She looked at the box, indicating he should go ahead and tend to its contents lest she die from anticipation.

'Well…?'

Having drawn the familiar-looking envelope from the box, he settled back making a show of tearing open the flap and nonchalantly flicking the page.

Raising the script to eye level, he began a word-for-word reading of the composition that he had himself put together only a day after his previous visit…

The chap was doing fine, or as fine as could be, alone in the Devonshire countryside with only the thoughts of his beloved's caresses to keep him company. Hyacinth giggled, clasping her hands and looking hard into Meredith's eyes.

'And…'

He made a show of reading slowly, labouring over references to the vastness of space, a plethora of 'darlings'. And – not forgetting to include a line about how he'd been spending his time, having had the wherewithal to recall Her Ladyship's parting enquiry in her previous letter.

He ruffled the page and turned to its closing lines…

Confirmation he was doing fine – spending his time as befits one stuck in the wilds of Devon – a few leisurely walks in the afternoons – good music, fine literature – a little light reading about the great cities of the world…Paris – Rome – Vienna!

He stopped to see Hyacinth sitting stiffly in her seat – her head held high, her lips pursed. Slowly, her face came to settle on Meredith's. She coughed twice and placed the cup on its saucer.

'Mr. Meredith. Let me get this right: walks in the afternoon. I think I'm hearing you correctly.'

Meredith stalled, something in the voice suggesting he might have overlooked some minor detail. He made a point of returning to the script, a quick check not seeming entirely out of place.

'Well, just the occasional walk, not every day obviously!' he added, quick to qualify the point with an attempt at jocularity. Hyacinth looked to the depths of the garden and immediately turned to catch Meredith's full attention.

'Mr. Meredith.' The cup was immediately placed on the table between them.

'It won't do – it simply won't do!' For a moment, it seemed tears of sadness – or maybe joy – were about to flow from the woman's eyes. She turned to Meredith.

'Mr. Meredith. Jacob is legless – both legs blown-off in a gas explosion in Montevideo. He hasn't put one foot in front of the other in seventeen years…'

She stared out of the window seeking what solace remained in the piles of junk awaiting the skip at the foot of the garden.

It was some time before she saw fit to turn in her seat and with her eye levelled at the seat opposite, reach to her smock – raising the petticoats and various undergarments to reveal what lay beneath – in her case…two unseemly stumps shrouded in folds of linen.

She looked hard at the expression peering blankly from behind a Garibaldi biscuit.

'Mr. Meredith. Do you really think two people – united by love and trust like myself and my beloved Jacob could even contemplate being apart were it feasible for things to be different?' She relaxed her grip on the skirts, the wafer-thin face relaxing just a fraction.

'It won't do Mr. Meredith. It simply won't do!' she said.

And then she turned again, the tiny eyes looking suddenly almost serene.

'Still – I suppose none of us is entirely innocent in these things,' she added with a sigh.

'Be not too alarmed. I think we both know that – unlike a stream – deceit can run in both directions. Do you understand what I am saying Mr. Meredith?'

Having abandoned the pretence on her side of the table, she brushed herself down and flattened her skirts to continue.

'So – Mr. Meredith...'

And – for a split second, it was as if nothing untoward had happened between them.

'In a minute my maid will place an envelope in your hand in which you'll find remuneration to the conclusion of your duties. I thank you for your work. All in all you have tended to your duties in a professional and business-like way.'

Meredith rose to his feet. She watched him brush his hat and reach quietly for his coat. It came as some relief to them both to have the pixie-woman put in her final appearance to present him with his parting envelope.

Back in the pub, a pint of 'Old' sitting on the table before him, there was ample time for reflection. Certainly – he could hardly have foreseen such a startling conclusion to his duties. Yet for all its unforeseen developments, a few taps on his calculator were quick to confirm that all had not been in vain; that even now – his afternoon pint sitting invitingly on the table before him – balancing debits against credits, he'd still be close to a four figure return for his endeavours, not bad for a few afternoons' work. And the bracing walks to and from the house had doubtless done him no harm. As his father would have put it: *For every door that slams shut, for sure another opens somewhere...*

A quick glance at his watch. One more here and a final one in the pub up the road.

Back in her ladyship's parlour the pixie-woman was in the process of gathering cups and plates on a tray. She caught her ladyship's disconsolate look.

'No good madam?' The trebly voice seemed to capture her employer's mood of deflation.

Hyacinth sighed and cocked a glance over her shoulder.

'Hopeless Deirdre – absolutely hopeless!'

There was an air of both resignation and irritation in the voice.

'I don't know where the agency gets them from Deirdre, I *really* don't.'

She turned to confirm the latest in a litany of shortcomings...

'Drab...absolutely drab...No eye for literature, the 'arts', no ear for music, no sporting tales to regale us with or adventures in foreign lands. Quite the saddest individual they've sent in ages.' She looked to her maid, her voice dropping an octave.

'Barely even an eye for matters physical, as far as I could make out.'

The pixie-woman rolled an eye whilst lifting the tray from its place on the table.

'So – not even a hint of a Jacob,' she said. Her Ladyship dismissed the comment with a sweep of the hand.

'As if from a different planet Deidre – an entirely different planet.' The pixie-woman sighed and took the tray firmly into her grasp.

'So which one was it madam – the gas explosion?'

Hyacinth nodded.

'Usually the best bet. Saves time and trouble...Now!'

She turned and with a clap of hands brought the pair of them back to business.

'There's another I believe. Due in about ten minutes, is that right?'

The maid nodded.

'And what's his name?'

'Carmichael madam: a youngster; they're getting younger every day! Something of a dapper dresser so I'm told – quite a dandy.'

'Hmm...We'll see Deirdre. We'll see. How about you – Devon okay or would you prefer a change of air?'

'No – Devon's fine,' the maid was quick to confirm, gratified to have been granted yet another reprieve – her position secured it seemed for a while yet. Nice train ride, quick jaunt in a local bus, few stiff walks across the moors.

It was some eight minutes later that the doorbell rang, and only a few minutes after that that Hyacinth half-turned to the disturbance behind her.

'You'll be Mr. Carmichael,' she said, the announcement struggling to make it through the miniscule aperture of her mouth.

The Curious Incidents Of The Writer At Night Time

Bacup Lawrence sat rubbing his hands, itching to get going with his next 'project'. But – first things first.

Before all else, a cup of coffee. How many cups he drank mattered not. When you're a writer you drink lots of coffee: the more the merrier. 'Good' writers...he knew about this because he's read about it and seen it on tv programmes...drink coffee to insane levels and smoke cigarettes to equally insane levels whilst working on their current 'projects'.

He poured more of the black liquid – 'black' because the best writers always drink their coffee black, and drank it slowly, allowing himself time to take in the subtle nuance of his surroundings: the objects and souvenirs he'd acquired over the years and placed around him in his study: things that seemed to say something about him as a person – a toy trumpet that he used to drive his parents crazy with as a kid, Arnold – his long droopy snake, designed to keep the draught from creeping under the door on those long winter nights, his plaster-cast of Chaucer – silent but often deadly once let loose in the public domain, and the main-man himself – Shakespeare glaring omnipotently from his marble plinth. And... the dreaded 'Lab-Top', peering hesitantly from its place on a neighbouring desk.... Ahh...How he hated the thing: cold, inanimate objects that have no part to play in the creative process: dealing with *real* feelings and *real* people!

He lit a cigarette. A glance at his watch told him it was already early morning. No worries! The later the better when settling down to write – the moment when a day begins to drift from the scene like the sails of a parting ship.

Another glug of coffee and the opportunity to mull over the all-important opening paragraph – the one whereby he would *hook* his reader, whilst guarding too against rushing into these things as if stacking cans of beans at his local supermarket! He was, after all, an *artist*...a *creator!* He would bide his time, waiting for his moment, and then pounce – like a lion leaping on its prey.

By which time, it was already eyes to the fore from the plinths and shelves around him.

'What's he up to?' whispered Arnold the snake, recoiling from his hidey-hole and watching their man perusing the magazine, searching for the spark that, in an instant, might galvanise him into action.

'Why, he's taking a quick shufti at one of the competition-winners in this month's Writing-Magazine. For there's no shame in seeking inspiration from the work of others,' explained Toy-Trumpet, extending his neck round a collection of *Penguin Modern Classics* to make himself heard.

Bacup was heard reading from the page....

Felicity struggled in desperation; her mind tormented, twisted like a severed cobra in the flimsiest of wicker baskets...

'God I hate you.' She spat the words like carpet tacks.

Looks were exchanged, eyebrows raised, all eyes coming to rest on Shakespeare smiling and muttering away to himself on his marble plinth.

'See how Shakespeare chuckles away to himself,' said Toy-Trumpet and Arnold in a single voice. The others rolled their eyes, Lab-Top shuffling his lid back and forth in an attempt to feel part of the action.

'For if he should lose a scruple of this sport let him be boiled to death in melancholy,' he said, shifting his way to the edge of the desk.'

'Shush Lab-Top,' said the others. 'Our man is psyching himself up in readiness to write.'

'And what do you know about scruples anyway?' said Pencil-Sharpener, somewhat pointedly and looking all superior from its place hooked to the side of the desk. 'For you are a cold inanimate object having no part to play in the creative process.'

'What I *do* know is…that creativity cannot be simply turned-on like a tap. It needs to be nurtured and constantly revised' said Lab-Top, somewhat huffily and far from ready to be entirely silenced in these matters. 'Was it John Updike who said *My ideas may come, but only where my pen has been and gone?*'

'Shut up Lab-Top,' came the cry – from all sides.

'Yes, shush…our man is deep in thought.'

Once more silence fell like a shroud as Bacup took another quick glug of coffee and leant pensively on his elbows. Even Shakespeare appeared momentarily sympathetic – himself more than familiar with the trials and tribulations of attempting to create something unique.

'*We write what we see, yet see only what we write*' he seemed to be saying, this time speaking entirely to himself.

It was another of this month's competition-winners that had drawn Bacup's attention….

As Jenna lifted her head her friend's voice broke like an explosion, a savage intrusion into her pain. Despite the sun streaming through the window she could barely make out the flowing locks of her friend's auburn hair as she stood gaunt and statuesque at her side.

Already we sense something stirring. Who is the 'friend'? Is she a 'friend' at all?

The author – Jennifer Allsop – says she set to explore the idea that friends aren't always what they appear to be.

There were tuts all round – Arnold shipping his tail up and down a few times and Pencil-Sharpener doing a few quick turns on the side of the desk.

'What's he up to now?' asked Toy-Trumpet, eyeing Lawrence suddenly thrust himself back in his seat, another cigarette snatched irritably from the packet on his desk.

'Likely asking himself those all-important questions,' suggested Arnold.

'Like – *Who* am I? *What* am I? Where exactly am I going with my work?' said Toy-Trumpet.

'What *exactly* am I trying to achieve?' said Arnold.

'And *why*?' added Lab-Top, still determined not to be entirely omitted from proceedings.

'Shut up Lab-Top,' came the reply. 'What do you know of what writers are trying to achieve?'

'Of *real* feelings and *real* people,' piped up Pencil-Eraser sidling up to Pencil-Sharpener sitting next to him on the desk.

'Or – maybe how to occupy himself once his task is done,' mused Toy-Trumpet. 'What befalls our man then? Plunge head-first into a sea of sorrows?'

'Mope back and forth across his accursed space losing track of all that holds a man together?' suggested Pencil-Eraser.

Questions, questions, questions.

'Well what then? What *is* our man about?' asked Arnold, his tail beginning to twitch at conversations that appeared to be heading nowhere.

'*Making sense of the world around him?*' suggested Shakespeare, who all were agreed tended to know about these things. It was a line they'd heard all writers come out with from time to time, and though not entirely sure what it meant it certainly had a ring to it.

'*Relating to the world around him?*' suggested Chaucer from his onyx plinth and to the accompaniment of such a huge rasping fart as had them all assured a thunderclappe must have erupted in the very skies above them.

'Shush,' said Toy-Trumpet, far from impressed by such discordant breaks of silence.

'Our man is trying to work,' cried Arnold, a finger drawn to miniscule lips. But maybe Chaucer had a point, for the line too carried a certain weightiness, if only in so far as no-one would be entirely able to grasp what it meant...

'What one actually *means* when one writes matters not a jot,' said Toy-Trumpet by way of explanation.

There were nods all round.

'The fact remains...few will understand what you're on about anyway,' added Arnold. 'You are after all *an observer of the human condition*...not a simple `story teller`...

Another quick drag from the cigarette and glance at his watch told their man it was 1:00am but he didn't care. Writers, especially good writers are often at their desk two, three, four, five-o-clock in the morning. It is the price one pays for being driven.

'See how he sits into the witching hours, like a man driven,' said Pencil-Sharpener.

'Was it Hemingway who said *The driver is more driven by the man than the man is driven by the driver...?* said Lab-Top.

'Shush Lab-Top. Our man is trying to write...'

'And think!' added Arnold.

In an instant Bacup was back to the magazine.

'Another quick shufti at this month's competition-winners,' whispered Toy-Trumpet to Arnold sitting aside him on the shelf. 'They must have been blessed with entries this month.'

'Roses For Rosaline'...by Michael Fairey.

'Two roses – small and fragile in the creeping sepia light of evening; their whispy aromas brushing gently against her olfactory lobes'...

A delicate tale of lost love, recrimination and guilt...Note: Two small roses – simple, delicate – untouched by the blight of deceit and despair.

There was a sudden distraction beneath them: a hint of movement beyond the pane of glass – or so it seemed. In a flash their man was at the window, gazing out into the darkness.

'Whoa who goes there? What creature stirs to quash a man's creative spirit? Is it the nightingale or is it the lark?'

'Or is it a bat?' put in Arnold, curling inquisitively round *Roget's Thesaurus* to Toy-Trumpet and flapping his tail impishly.

'Or some other creature-of-the-night striving to make its mark of the canvas of a new day?' suggested Pencil-Eraser, whispering covertly and speaking mainly to Pencil-Sharpener still perched next to him on the side of the desk.

But then, within seconds their man was back at his desk – head-bowed and raring to go, the fire of creativity suddenly burning like hot coals springing forth from the very jaws of Hell!

'See – our man, he is at it!' cried Arnold.

'That sudden burst of inspiration,' cried Toy-Trumpet.

Even the pot-elephant who rarely made any contribution to what he saw around him seemed flummoxed to see their man so suddenly overcome and thrust into such a frenzy of activity...

'Our man is certainly inspired,' it whispered to a plastic gnome sitting aside a jam-jar on the shelf.

'Of what does our fellow write? Asked a tiny troll, stepping along the shelf to get in on the action for a while.

'Who can say what spurs a man to write?' put in Toy-Trumpet, casting a sidelong glance at the others and particularly at Lab-Top simmering quietly on the periphery of all the action.

'The vagaries of unrequited love?' suggested Pencil-Sharpener.

'Or that thing about 'love' forever falling between two stools, as in a tug-of-war,' suggested Plastic Gnome.

'Shut up Gnome,' said the others. 'What do plastic gnomes know about such things as 'love'?

'Or 'love' as a kind of paradox; the thing we strive for being the very thing that stops us from achieving it,' added Troll, peering from his place behind the line of *Encyclopaedia Britannica's*.

There were nods and sympathetic looks on all sides.

'Was it Saul Bellow who said *There is only so much to pour from my heart as will fit in the barrel of my fountain-pen?*' asked Lab-Top still sulking yet equally determined not to be construed as putting a complete lid on proceedings.

'Quiet Lab-Top,' piped up the others. 'For you are but a cold inanimate object, having no part to play in the creative process...

'Dealing with *real* feelings...'

'And *real* people!'

And all at once – as silence fell – it seemed the questions had gone: either already answered or as irrelevant as they were once pressing as their man first took his place at his desk.

For what is this man who suddenly toils at his desk like the blacksmith hammering away at his anvil?

He is a writer...

'Just a guy trying to make sense of the world around him,' said Toy-Trumpet.

'Or relating to the world around him,' said Gnome.

'Or – a man *embarking on a journey that might yet turn out to be an engaging metaphor for the life-long search for the inner-self*,' said Lab-Top.

'Shut up Lab-Top,' they all said.

'What do you know about engaging metaphors?'

'Or the life-long search for the inner-self?'

'For you are but a_____'

Edwin's Little Secret

Edwin Matlock's route to the shop was, by now, a familiar one. It would take him along Argyle Avenue to the lights, first right and then a few hundred yards to Trafalgar Gardens where he would catch a bus taking him close to the centre of town. From there he would walk the eighty or so yards to the shop's door, crossing at the green-man next Dale's bakery and patisserie.

It was at the beginning of July that his mother had sat him down to follow her finger as she indicated the route that would get him safely to the bus-stop, the points for crossing the road and the exact bus stop to wait at until the bus came to a halt. The importance of catching the bus at this point could not be overstated, and accordingly the spot had been circled with a red pen with the approaching road similarly highlighted.

The decision to allow Edwin to do three hours work twice a week in Mr. Grimshaw's shop had not been taken lightly, and was based on three basic assumptions: *One* It would get him out of the house for a few hours each day, thus enabling him to be a little independent – getting to the bus stop each day and paying his fare to the driver. *Two*...he would gain some sense of responsibility and much needed practice at basic arithmetic from working the till. *Three*...it would get him from under his mother's feet for a while, thus awarding her a few hours much-earned breathing space.

Her husband, whose inclination was to leave such arrangements to his wife, had little reason (or motivation) to question the decision, and the agreement to have him work in the shop had been delivered in writing some three weeks prior to him actually arriving on the scene; Mr. Grimshaw's thinking – that it would save him a few bob whilst pursuing one or two other little avenues – either conveniently overlooked or omitted entirely from the equation.

Though a forbidding and at times overbearing woman, Edwin's mother's adopted view of the world was relatively simple and straightforward: that it, or more accurately, those who inhabited it, slotted conveniently into two camps: there was *good* and there was *bad*: less a measured appraisal than a means of steering her children (particularly her eldest child) into what was deemed to be a more productive direction.

It was Edwin's fortune to be greeted by examples of what was inherently 'good' each and every morning as he took his place at the breakfast table: his mother, Charlotte Matlock, spooning beans next to two rashers of bacon. His father, Gerald Matlock, skipping through his paper, *The Daily Telegraph* and sipping tea. His sister, Geraldine Matlock, burrowing a spoon into a bowl of Rice-Krispies, the spoon gripped like a broom-handle in her tiny fist.

All of which, though maybe valid as passing observation, failed to take into account an equally valid and – as far as Edwin was concerned – far more pressing consideration: that things are apt to be less straightforward if you happen to be *fat* – or 'severely overweight' as his mother sometimes chose to term it.

Being fat – or severely overweight – brought problems that only Edwin and other fat, or overweight, kids could ever appreciate: problems having less to do with *good, bad – right* and *wrong,* than more urgent matters such as school, parents, and particularly over-zealous relatives whose habit was to arrive at the most untoward times of the week with the sole purpose of squeezing his cheeks and pointing out – in case he wasn't aware of the fact – that he was growing up fast – ie... that he was getting 'fat'. Had he been tall and skinny no-one would have been remotely interested because when you're tall and skinny such things either don't happen or just don't matter. It is only when you are fat, or severely overweight, that such things get noticed, and the more 'lovable' you are deemed to be. Which was an irony, considering that for the bulk of his adolescent years Edwin was lonely, isolated and generally miserable.

Which maybe went some way to explaining the shop coming onto the scene.

For it was here that for a few hours each day Edwin was able to escape the bleak world into which he had been thrust for far more engaging worlds to be found in the stack of comics Mr. Grimshaw had acquired over the years and placed obligingly under his nose in the shop: a world of super-heroes and arachnid monsters, death-ray machines and spider-slayers, a world where *good, bad, right* and *wrong* all played their part, but in ways that seemed to make more sense than in the far more daunting world beyond the comics' pages.

This was Edwin's world and for a few hours during the course of a typical afternoon there would be little to distract him from it. Customers came, customers went; a few browsed, a few hovered, a few bought fishing mags or musty old books written by mostly dead people. Some wandered the aisles looking for something they were reasonably sure they'd never find – whilst others were there with no other purpose than to kill a bit of time: all people with time on their hands, rarely a word to say, and – much like Edwin – in search of temporary refuge from the hurly-burly of life beyond its walls.

Edwin had negotiated the bus-ride, crossed the road at the appropriate point, and by late afternoon a relatively uneventful day appeared to be heading for an equally uneventful conclusion, culminating in a five-o-clock sweep along both aisles of the shop and a quick check out back: a small area at the rear of the shop where Mr. Grimshaw kept copies of things in reserve: piles of things even more boring than half the stuff in the shop itself – boxes of old-fashioned novels, encyclopaedias, piles of 'Knitting Today', 'World-At Wars', all destined for an early grave and likely thankful for it.

It was shortly after five-o-clock whilst sweeping at the rear of the shop that Edwin happened to clap eyes on a pile of old reading material stuck in the corner, some in boxes, but some just sitting there on the floor unnoticed – what appeared to be old magazines rather than books, likely undisturbed for years.

Maybe it was the idea of them simply sitting there gathering dust that got him thinking – that his pile of comics out front of the shop wouldn't last forever. And that maybe there'd be more of the same, just sitting there in the corner waiting to be discovered, possibly some titles he'd never even heard of. Certainly, there'd be no harm in having a look.

Putting the broom to one side and struggling to get himself down on his haunches, he began fumbling his way through the top half dozen copies, succeeding, at first, in discovering little beyond a few decades of dust. Other than that, nothing – just a few railway mags, half a dozen 'National Geographic's. He scooped a little further, craning his neck like you do when you're trying to read something you can't quite get at. A few on stamps and coins, a few army manuals, after which the pile took a bit of manoeuvring. It was strange how awkward a pile of magazines could be to shift, even from side to side.

Making a concerted effort, he made a grab at a few corners underneath and pulled, at first gently and then with a bit more force, easing them this way and that, until eventually – with a little cooperation from the pile – a small wad of magazines came sliding into his hand.

He glanced at the top cover and instinctively looked away. Only when he'd collected himself sufficiently did he dare look again.

There were two women on the cover of the magazine – young women; but more than that – they had no clothes on!

His immediate thought, and the sensible thing to do would be to stuff the magazines back – get them back exactly where they had come from, get up, brush himself down and get back to the front of the shop. But he didn't. Instead, he did his usual thing of huffing and puffing. And then for some reason – call it schoolboy curiosity or the realisation that for a few moments at least, he was alone in the shop; moments during which no-one would have the faintest inkling of what he was up to – he hesitated. Managing to shut all thoughts of things beyond the shop out of his mind, he allowed himself a quick sneak at the top cover; and moments later, found himself leafing through the opening pages.

Each page – a similar story: more women, all naked, some full of smiles, some clutching beach-balls, one or two lying in the grass holding hands. Another page. This time two women, both with nothing on and one with a foot raised on a tree-trunk. Both were smiling at the camera.

Another magazine; this one's title a word he didn't understand – some word ending *us* like a foreign word. Inside the cover, two more women with nothing on kneeling in front of men's privates which were long and seemed to be pointing in the direction of a clump of trees.

It was as he was in the process of turning the page to where two friends were about to join them, that the bell above the shop door rang and seconds later – footsteps sounded somewhere inside the door.

'Edwin?' It was Mr. Grimshaw's voice.

Edwin leapt back, grabbing the bag at his side and wrenching it apart sufficient to stuff the wad of magazines inside.

'Edwin!' The voice was louder now, impatient at catching no sight of the boy in his customary place behind the counter.

It was as a wizened face appeared in the space between the rear and front of the shop that Edwin yanked the bag's string and stood almost as if to attention.

'Ah – there y' are.' The voice had dropped a tone at finding the boy about his duties as expected.

'Alright then?' Edwin sniffled and just about managed to nod.

Mr. Grimshaw watched him shuffle from foot to foot. Though he didn't appear to be up to any mischief he seemed a bit flustered. But then again, he often seemed a bit flustered.

He repeated the question, rotating his chin which was a habit of his when facing an issue he wasn't quite sure how to tackle.

'You finished in 'ere? You done 't floor?'

Edwin managed another nod and blinked at the broom leaning against the shelf.

'Well come on then.' Mr. Grimshaw knew there were times when Edwin needed to be gee'd along a little. 'Let's be 'avin' you.'

Edwin had little choice than to comply, slinking his way through the gap into the main part of the shop, the bag clutched over his shoulder, desperate to avoid it becoming a focal point of attention.

'So, you've tidied up, swept up. Take much?'

Edwin turned his back on the counter and shook his head.

'No well...' Mr. Grimshaw was still watching the boy.

'Right – I'll see to 't rest. You can bugger off now.'

He continued to watch Edwin pull the strap more firmly and look nervously in the direction of the window.

Mr. Grimshaw, reading the situation, allowed his gaze to follow him onto the street.

'Your mother's coming to get yer is she?'

Edwin jolted at the prospect but could only nod, and try not to think about it. What he mustn't do was cry; crying rarely helped; experiences at school had told him that; if anything it just made things worse.

What he *did* know was that at that moment he would have done anything or given anything to have the clocks turn back – just fifteen minutes; enough to have everything back in its rightful place: Mr. Grimshaw still out on his rounds, him sweeping harmlessly up and down the aisles, the magazines sitting undisturbed in the corner.

It was some time later, that Mr. Grimshaw, having positioned himself by the window, nodded towards the road.

'This your mother?'

Edwin watched the familiar shape of his mother's car draw up a few yards along the pavement, and moments later, an equally familiar figure emerge from it and step onto the pavement.

Mr. Grimshaw appeared to grimace too as he opened the door for Mrs. Matlock to step across the threshold. He didn't know Edwin's mother too well – but well enough.

'Ah. Mr. Grimshaw,' she said, quick to acknowledge the man's *logo-parentis* responsibility for Edwin during the boy's afternoon hours. She removed a pair of sharp leather gloves and made a point of familiarising herself with the shop's interior layout.

'And how are you Mr. Grimshaw; keeping well I trust?' It was a habit of Edwin's mother in the company of strangers to both put questions and answer them in the same breath: a means of keeping a step ahead of proceedings and confirmation that their engagement was to be kept brief and to the point. 'And your wife; is she well?' Mr. Grimshaw shuffled his way to begin sorting out the till, confirming that she, indeed the pair of them, were doing fine.

'Good. Now, come on Edwin. We need to get back. Stop, look, check. Do you have everything with you?'

As often in the presence of others, his mother's voice seemed to acquire a particularly shrill quality, on this occasion sufficient to have Edwin shrink more visibly, his unease – as ever – failing to register as she quickly straightened her gloves and turned to go, pausing only to have something positive said about her son.

'And tell me – are you happy with Edwin's contribution? How is he faring?' Mr. Grimshaw reassured her he was doing fine, already having crossed the shop to open the door to facilitate both their exits.

'Good. Edwin say goodnight to Mr. Grimshaw, and thank him for allowing you to work at the shop.'

Edwin obliged on both counts, stepping onto the pavement, his mother clutching one hand, the other hand clutching the strap of the shoulder-bag firmly across his shoulder.

Once in the car he quickly shuffled the bag between his legs. His mother waited, watching him settle into place before following suit beside him, hesitating a moment before starting the ignition.

Being far from a vivacious boy – the slightest hint of him being a little out-of-sorts was sufficient to draw attention.

'Edwin, is everything all right?' His mother was peering in the mirror attempting to have the question come across as more routine than might be intended. Edwin nudged the bag further between his feet. It failed to divert her attention.

She looked down, checking he hadn't somehow got his feet tangled in the car's foot controls.

Edwin knew that look. And again unwittingly nudged the bag, immediately fretting about being questioned as to why he kept playing with his bag.

His mother looked aggrieved.

'If you've been spending your money on sweets I'd much rather you told me,' she said finally, looking across the few feet between them and sighing at once again finding herself compelled to answer her own question.

Having been handed a reprieve, albeit a temporary one, Edwin was wise enough to leave the bag for a moment, and to hang his head: a tactic he occasionally adopted when the odds seemed particularly stacked against him – on this occasion forcing him to look up as his mother clamped two hands firmly on the steering wheel. She was not happy, and saw it as her responsibility to make it clear why.

'Edwin. You've disappointed me.' As often there was as much an air of resignation as genuine anger in the voice. She drew the car to a halt at the set of lights and again directed her gaze at the mirror.

'You see Edwin, there are additives in sweets, not to mention the artificial colourings and sugars that to an overweight boy – an obese boy – can spell disaster. Do you understand what I'm saying?'

Edwin nodded.

'Good.'

'As long as you didn't spend all your money.' Edwin felt himself subjected to another reproachful look.

He shook his head, the holdall sitting idly between his feet.

Only when his mother drew the car into their driveway and brought it to a halt did the enormity of his plight strike home; his mother's voice, for once, reduced to little more than background blur.

She withdrew the key and placed it in the right side of her handbag. It was as Edwin began the process of extracting himself from his seat, that his mother drew him back a moment.

'So – what lessons have we learnt today Edwin?'

Another familiar routine, on this occasion highlighting the fact that while we all make mistakes, none of us is beyond redemption.

'Not to tell fibs and not to eat sweets,' he said, eager to be indoors before his mother started pressing him on where he might have put the sweets he hadn't eaten.

'And not to forget letting down your mother,' she added, snapping the handbag shut.

Edwin nodded and reached for the handle.

'And don't forget your bag,' she added finally.

Only once indoors and having made it to the sanctuary of his room did the hopelessness of the situation finally sink in. Not so much deceiving his mother or telling fibs, but the far more alarming prospect of having magazines full of naked women sitting alongside him in his room.

A realisation that had him dump the bag to one side and slump on the bed.

Getting rid of them was the obvious thing to do, but how? He couldn't just put them in the bin. His mother would be certain to spot the sudden appearance of a plastic-bag full of magazines, even stuffed under empty tins and egg-shells. Taking them away from the house to be dumped was a possibility. But again – how? He wasn't allowed out at night, and where was the nearest bin? How did he explain himself – a holdall slung over his shoulder – to a policeman doing his rounds? He had a vision of being brought home in a police car, the collection of magazines waved in front of his mother's face: 'Don't worry Mrs Matlock, we've got your son's magazines, right here in this bag!' He immediately dismissed any such idea.

His next appearance in the shop would be the day after tomorrow. Maybe he could take them back to the shop and replace them in the pile. It would mean standing next to his mother in the hall kissing her on the cheek with the magazines sitting in the bag slung over his shoulder, but what else could he do? Kiss her and *then* get the bag? Then she'd want to know why he'd gone to get the bag after he'd kissed her. Maybe he wouldn't have to kiss her. Again hardly likely. She insisted on being kissed. Mothers always insisted on being kissed, when anyone went anywhere.

Another possibility that hadn't escaped him was Mr. Grimshaw maybe discovering the magazines had gone missing, though that seemed unlikely. More likely was him not even knowing they were there, ironically making them officially, or maybe unofficially, Edwin's property – a bizarre notion in itself. And even if he did notice, what could he say without drawing unwanted attention?

But – all that was for the future; what he needed now was temporary storage space, somewhere inside the house.

He looked round and considered a few possibilities. Under the stairs was another non-starter – too full of coats and bottles of his father's homemade wine and too little space to hide them in. In fact the whole of downstairs was out of the question. The garage? There was an old chest of drawers out there full of nuts and bolts and old paint brushes, but it was strictly his father's territory. Were he to be discovered skulking amongst boxes of nails and screws explanations would certainly be demanded. Another option – his sister's room! It was the only room that had a kind of cubby-hole complete with its own shelves and a door. He knew there was junk in there going back years; the possibility of stuffing the magazines under the whole lot of it was not inconceivable – only the idea of actually doing it was inconceivable. A vision of his sister descending the stairs, the magazines clutched in her tiny fist sufficient to put paid to that one.

There was only one answer – what control of the situation he had, he needed to hang onto; the only solution was to keep them in his own room.

Seated midst a renewed wave of panic, he loosened the bag and tipped it onto the bed, compelled to witness the offending articles tumbling into vision, the top cover – two girls sitting naked on blanket. He grabbed the magazines and in a hurried attempt to dismiss them at least temporarily from sight – and mind – leant across the bed to stuff them under his pile of *Marvels*, *Dandys* and *Beano-Bumper-Book-Of-Fun*.

It came as some relief to hear the call to wash his hands and prepare for tea.

Edwin's contribution to mealtimes was to take the condiments to the table and place them in the centre, next to the jug of water and the glasses.

Upon taking their seats, it was hands together, eyes closed. After which his mother eased the tray of vegetables towards her husband.

It was not the occasion for breaking any of the rules when it came to eating his tea. Only one scoop of potato, no leaving the pie spoon in the peas dish, no slouching in his chair and to remember the smaller knife was for buttering bread to go with soup, even though there wasn't any soup. Why the smaller knives were put out when there was no soup was never made clear. When there *was* soup, tomato was his favourite though he had to be careful not to spill it in his lap. He also knew not to talk whilst chewing his food.

Not that he would have had much to say, nor later whilst taking his turn drying the dishes. Or later still, whilst watching tv.

It was during the hours that followed; empty drifting hours – time paying little regard to issues that already seemed to have ventured well beyond his control – that he yearned for it to be the same as any other evening: a scene already fixed firmly in his memory where nothing even remotely eventful or out of the ordinary seemed destined to happen: the tv flickering harmlessly in one corner, his father dozing in an opposite corner, his mother drifting in and out of consciousness on the chair opposite, his sister absently colouring away in her Animal-A-Day colouring book – a state-of-play which, till now, he had rarely given much thought, but on this occasion seemed more agreeable than anything he could ever have imagined.

It was only later, with the evening's transition into night-time all but complete, that the realisation dawned that the scene being played out before him was – to all intents – exactly that; that not one of them had the faintest notion that at that very moment a few feet above their heads stood a stack of magazines full of pictures of naked women!

And with it, the equally startling realisation that it was going to make not a jot of difference to anyone's evening. That what was happening – right here in this room or on the shelves a few feet above it – was his secret and his alone.

For the first time in his life Edwin had the strange sensation of feeling he was somehow in control!

Above all else it brought passive acceptance of the rituals of bed-time – a peck on his mother's cheek, a promise to clean both sides of his teeth, to seek forgiveness for his wrongdoings, and a commitment to avoid repeating them.

And then, later still – a further commitment – to lie in bed staring hard at the shadows cast behind a partly closed door, waiting for the sound of footsteps on the stairs, confirmation that the landing-light was about to be extinguished – the official close-of-play in the Matlock household.

And then an even longer wait; waiting for faint whispers from next door to finally subside, reassured that only a few feet away – the girls would be waiting too, already gathered in ones and twos, some standing in fields or huddled round garden-gates – confirmation that that though his secret was safe, it was down to him to ensure it remained so.

It was exactly on the half hour that – having convinced himself that whatever wrongdoings were about to occur would be adequately concealed beneath the sheets of his bed – he raised himself on his elbows, listening again for any lingering signs of activity next door, and upon hearing nothing, reached down and fingered his way along the bottom shelf to the hard back cover of his *Beano-Bumper Book Of Fun* – and then beneath, to where the recent additions to the pile lay undisturbed from earlier – grabbing their corners and drawing them slowly from the pile.

Magazines in hand, the next step was to ease himself back into place, pulling the sheet and blanket towards his shoulders and turning himself onto his side. Twisting round he took hold of the small torch, a birthday-gift from his Uncle Norman, and lowered it under the blanket. Only then did he join it, raising the sheet and blanket over his head, effectively creating a mini-tent around him. And only then daring to switch the torch on. In an instant, the whole inside of his bed was cast in a blinding yellow light.

Top of the pile was *Nature's True Course*. And then the ones with the foreign sounding titles. Getting them into a sort of pile he was back to *Nature's True Course* – two women standing each side of a tennis net, holding hands and tennis-rackets in their other hands. Both were completely naked. Edwin stared – intrigued at the way women looked with no clothes on, particularly under torchlight last thing at night beneath the sheets of his bed. The only female he'd ever seen with no clothes on was his sister when she was a baby, but that didn't count. Slowly – determined not to miss out on the slightest detail – he started turning the pages.

Edwin had never kissed a girl – aside from his sister and his cousins, but that didn't count either – a 'kiss' as in...on-the-lips, not on the cheek. He had thought about it on numerous occasions with regard to Jasmine Mc. Nulty and Sarah Entwistle at school, though thinking about it was as far as he'd got, or was likely to get. The chances of actually doing it to either of them were nil. Girls, or at least the pretty ones, tended not to kiss boys who were fat – or severely overweight – or ugly; and he had the distinct impression he qualified on all three counts.

The girl with her foot raised on the tree-trunk was neither fat nor severely overweight, and was certainly not ugly – and, Edwin decided, bore close resemblance to Jasmine Mc. Nulty. All of which pointed to the fact she was aching to be kissed. In fact, they were *all* aching to be kissed, every single one of them. You could see it in their eyes, in their faces, in their poses lying naked in the grass or against trees or leaning over fences.

Shifting on his side, Edwin extinguished the torch and eased the magazine into position, emerging momentarily to confirm his movements remained undetected.

With everyone – himself, the girls and more than likely his parents next door – finally engulfed in darkness and the girls already in position beside him, he closed his eyes and lowered his head to plant a firm kiss on the smooth glossy paper, allowing his lips to linger a moment before re-emerging from beneath the blanket: *one* to gauge the effect of kissing a girl for the first time and *two* checking the sounds of people kissing in the adjacent room hadn't disturbed his mother.

There was little to report. It seemed his secret was safe, and for the time being at least, set to remain so.

Dipping his head back to where the girls continued to wait patiently, he manoeuvred the magazine back into position and lowered his head a second time – relishing the feel of warm lips brushing against cool paper, first one kiss, then another, turning the page to where another girl – this one bearing close resemblance to Sarah Entwistle – stood or lay naked in the darkness. He lowered his head to meet her, this time with his mouth slightly open like he'd sometimes seen couples on tv kiss the moment before his mother reached for the remote-control.

It was several pages into the third magazine that *Nature's True Course* was to take a whole new direction, convincing Edwin that his secret was safe enough to have him divest himself of his pyjamas and join the girls, placing his own version of blubbery nakedness next to *pages twelve and thirteen* of *Nexus – Volume Three's...Fountain Frolics – Summertime Splashes In The Park!*

With eyes now clamped firmly shut he drew the open magazine onto his chest – relishing the feel of cool velvety paper sliding across the warm flab of his belly, venturing lower and then lower still, until – on reaching what appeared to be the point of no return and with visions of naked girls spread-eagled on the grass before him – he began to rotate the magazine; a steady rhythmic rotation that grew bolder and stronger, until – at some vague point and without any hint of a warning it came to a shuddering halt – leaving Edwin gasping for breath, the girls no doubt the same – their hearts likely beating as violently as his own.

It was in the cold light of day that the harsh realities of life were there to greet him once more, slumping him against the pillow, his eye and thoughts drifting to where the girls had been safely tucked away back in their place on the shelf.

A sterner test awaited, in light of which Edwin found himself thrust into a far from untypical post-breakfast lull: a listless wandering from room to room in what his mother referred to as one of his 'loitering moods': hanging around, doing nothing and generally getting under her feet, thereby making a nuisance of himself. On this occasion prompting the suggestion that with day outside looking reasonably welcoming, why not take himself out into it; maybe get himself down the park and go on the swings and watch the ducks.

The suggestion caught Edwin entirely off-guard – the thought immediately crossing his mind: was he being presented with an opportunity to get rid of the magazines, or at least some of them? To remove them from the scene by ditching them in a bin at the park? Placing himself by the door he gave it a moment's thought. A possibility, yet one still riddled with complications, like his mother wanting to know why he was taking his bag. And even if she didn't ask, the idea of standing face to face with her in the hall with the bag full of magazines slung over his shoulder – too appalling a prospect to even consider. Apart from anything, he'd never get away with it. After yesterday she might even search his bag to check he wasn't telling fibs. It was one of her golden rules – not to tell fibs.

He struggled into his duffle-coat. The magazines would remain where they were, at least for now. He buttoned up his coat and reached to kiss his mother with a promise not to buy ice-cream, go too high on the swings and to walk swiftly in the opposite direction if approached by older men – or women.

There were no women of any description in this part of the park, or men. Just a few kids milling around on the swings, shouting and kicking a football back and forth across the concrete play-area. Two girls approached strolling arm in arm, making a point of giggling in an exaggerated manner, eyeing Edwin contemptuously when close enough and dissolving in fits of giggles once beyond him.

The ducks too were relatively low-key, fanning out from the side and gliding across the water like a flotilla of toy yachts. Edwin sat on the bench, as intrigued as ever at the way not one of them seemed inclined to set a foot out of place or head off in a different direction. To his right, a stretch of park beyond an ice-cream van was dotted with people, some in groups, some strolling in twos and threes, some hand-in-hand. He stared after them, eyeing the miniscule stirrings of activity – teenagers sprawled in the grass, couples strolling the length of the lakeside. He thought about the girls in the magazines sprawled in the grass, some of them strolling hand-in-hand past lines of trees or leaning against five-barred-gates – his thoughts interrupted by another group of girls, in this case passing close by on the path clad in smart yellow jump-suits, wires dangling from each ear. Maybe it was once again finding himself midst a flurry of female activity that had him turn his attention back to the road.

Back in the house little had changed, a distant humming from somewhere, the groan of the washing machine out in the garage. There seemed little need to announce his return. Interrupting his mother in the midst of her household chores wasn't always the wisest move.

Succeeding in negotiating the first two stairs in a single leap, he made his way to the landing, pushing the door to his room open and waiting a moment, checking to see whether his return had been noted. There was nothing beyond the faint hum of a vacuum cleaner.

He entered the room, faltering at the sight of his bed having been made, his shirt for tomorrow hanging on its hanger. Without hesitation, he leapt across the bed, reaching for the bottom shelf, sifting through the pile – and coming to a stop far sooner than he'd have expected. He tried again, almost counting his way down, corner by corner to the hard-back book, again venturing beneath only to make contact only with the surface of the shelf. Once again, this time leaning further to follow each movement of his fingers. Still nothing! Just a hard flat surface beneath his *Beano Bumper Book Of Fun*…The magazines had disappeared!

He could do no more than throw himself back onto the bed.

Inevitably – and irrevocably – the tears came: tears that stung his eyes and burned his face: tears that would likely go on forever and were for things he would never be able to fully explain – things his mother would never know about, nor likely want to know about. Whilst somewhere, a million miles beneath him, the drone of the vacuum-cleaner was the only sound to be heard.

A sound that a few moments later, was broken by a call from below. His return had been noted after all.

'Edwin!'

Footsteps followed the voice, eager to investigate the apparent lack of a reply. Edwin lay flat, quite unable to move. Seconds later his mother appeared at the door.

'Ah – there you are.' She was watching him closely, searching for signs of acknowledgement. And quickly clapping her hands.

'Come on. Get your coat. We're going into town.'

Edwin looked up, his face peppered with tiny scars, his eyes raw.

'Come on – chop chop!' She seemed strangely insistent – no doubt as aware as anyone there were times when her son needed to be geed along a little.

Dazed and hopelessly confused, Edwin drew himself to his feet, the streaks down his face filling every quarter of the room.

'Come on – get your bag,' his mother repeated, an edge to her voice that Edwin had rarely, if ever, heard before.

Together they descended the stairs and without another word being uttered left the house, Edwin clutching his mother's hand, the other hand clutching his bag tightly over his other shoulder.

On leaving the house nothing was said, nor would be said – not in the hours, days, weeks, months that would follow – about the events of the last twenty-four hours.

It was – as Edwin might reflect if he was able to at some point – destined to remain just another of life's great insoluble secrets!

The Issue Of A Mat Being Placed On The Front Outside Step

[A sequel to *The Issue Of A Lever Being Attached To The Rear Outside Door* in the previous book…'Call These Stories']

There'd been little to write home about in terms of goings-on in and around the building. Something of a surprise then when Harold And Jean from Flat Two arrived home from one of their three weekly shopping expeditions to find a mat had been put on the step leading up to the entrance to the block: actually *on* the step, as in: you had the path leading up to the step, then the step, then the door.

The pair grounded their shopping a moment and stopped to examine the mat a little more closely. It appeared to be a regular sort of mat, the kind you see on steps of buildings the length and breadth of the country; in this case with a neat green and red interwoven pattern fanning out from the centre of one side in a kind of Chinese-fan effect, which led to a quite distinctive and rather unusual feature – the mat was semi-circular in shape. ie. a straight edge up against the side of the step and a semi-circular shape fanning round the step itself.

Harold and Jean exchanged looks. It definitely hadn't been there when they'd left to go shopping which meant it must have been placed there between eleven-o-clock and one-thirty. They did a quick check on their watches just to check they'd got their times right.

Harold ventured a foot onto the mat. It was tufty and a bit springy – solid-enough looking and, they both noticed, bordered by a thin black rubber perimeter, probably designed to protect the mat from damage or to prevent it from getting frayed. Interestingly, neither of them had noticed the black perimeter at first, indication of it blending reasonably well with the rest of the mat, which was a kind of horsy-brown colour.

Jean asked Harold how wide he thought the mat was and Harold said he thought it was maybe two to two-and-a-half feet wide, or long, depending on which way you look at it. It was difficult to be precise when you're standing up and the mat's on the step beneath your feet.

The question was – who had put the mat on the step? It was difficult to say. Some time ago when a lever had appeared on the rear outside door they'd guessed it was Tom because with Tom being a bit of a handyman it had Tom written all over it, but – then again – maybe it hadn't been Tom. But when it came to putting a mat on the step it could be anyone. So the question remained – who would be more likely to put a mat on the step?

The logical move was to contact Marilyn in Flat Ten.

Back in their flat Harold rang Marilyn's number. Marilyn answered the phone and Harold put her in the picture: that a semi-circular mat about two to two-and-a-half feet wide had appeared on the step of the left-side front entrance some time between eleven-o-clock and one-thirty. Marilyn was immediately reminded of the lever appearing on the rear outside door and the previous October – a picture of flying-fish appearing on the wall of the communal entrance area. Again, an obvious question, one that Marilyn was herself quick to ask – who could have put the mat on the step?

It was agreed that it might be worth going across to have a look at the mat, but given that it was something they'd *all* be standing on, as opposed to pictures of flying fish that some of them may, or may not, look at, maybe a few of the others could be invited to join them. Harold agreed that it made sense and phoned Ken in Flat Seven and Edna and her husband Jim in Flat Nine. Jim was out but Edna was in and agreed to pop down to have a look at the mat along with Ken.

Their arrival pretty much coincided. Jean and Harold were there too as they were the ones who'd discovered the mat on arrival back home from shopping.

Standing in a semi-circle round the mat they were each able to give it a thorough viewing. All were agreed it was a solid-enough looking mat and Marilyn and Ken ventured a foot to test for springiness. Harold, having set foot on it earlier, was able to confirm that he too had found it fairly springy and pointed out the black rubber border to protect it from fraying – a feature the others, except for Tom – who tended to notice these things – had missed on initial viewing.

The question (apart from – who could have put it there) was what to do about it?

The logical move was to hold a meeting in Marilyn's flat. Later that day Marilyn would send the missives round, updating everyone on the situation and inviting everyone to the meeting. They decided to invite everyone as on the last occasion – when a lever had been attached to the rear outside door – some residents had taken exception at being excluded from the meeting on the grounds of not being directors and thus denied the opportunity to comment. There seemed no logical reason why only directors should have a point of view when it came to levers being attached to doors. Marilyn had pointed out it was to do with numbers but in order to keep the peace had agreed to extend an open-invitation should another lever appear on one of the doors – though in this case it was a mat appearing on a step as opposed to a lever appearing on a door.

In the meantime Ken would check with the lease to see what it had to say about mats appearing on doorsteps and report back to the meeting.

The agendas went out later that day.

The meeting would be in Marilyn's flat at ten-o-clock the following morning, but it was agreed that a communal viewing of the mat prior to the meeting might be a good idea, so they agreed to meet not in Marilyn's flat, but on the doorstep of the neighbouring entrance at…let's say nine-fifty, ten minutes beforehand, allowing time to examine the mat and formulate ideas in advance of the meeting itself.

A number of residents turned up at around nine-forty five. First to arrive, Hilary from flat eight followed by Tom from flat five, who, being arguably the most practical-minded amongst them, was immediately on his knees testing for springiness and likely resistance to general wear and tear, confirming on rising to his feet, that it seemed sufficiently robust to withstand whatever number of feet were likely to be stepping on and off it in the course of a typical day.

Harold raised the issue of its shape – semi-circular as opposed to rectangular, but as Marilyn pointed out, why discuss the mat's shape now when they'd soon be in a meeting where it would be raised formally? There was general agreement and on looking at his watch, Jim pointed out it was almost time for the meeting to start so maybe they should make their way to Marilyn's flat.

Once in her flat, Tom agreed to do the minutes and Marilyn thanked him for that and for the others for attending the meeting which, she confirmed, was to discuss the sudden appearance of a mat on the step of the left side main entrance to the building.

First up was Ken who put them in the picture regarding the rules and regulations pertaining to *accessibility with reference to communal areas* in so far as *quick and ready* access must be maintained at all times. It was less specific as to the issue of actually placing a mat on the step.

So – *quick and ready* access. General consensus appeared to be that with the mat being *on* the ground, unlike the lever that had been fixed to the rear outside door, access was largely unaffected; unless, as Jean pointed out, one wanted to take into account the slight springy effect of the mat which could conceivably propel you towards the door a little quicker. It was agreed that whilst this was a valid point, it would be difficult to gauge. And may vary according residents' weight, Tom pointed out. Which may be true, but it would be a brave man or woman who saw fit to pass comment on the weight and shape of fellow residents!

Marilyn thanked Jean for that, at which point Harold raised a hand to bring them to the issue of the shape of the mat, but Marilyn pointed out they'd be coming to that in item three, item two being where the mat had been placed – ie. actually *on* the step. And asked Harold whether he had a thing about the shape of mats!

There were chuckles as Harold hung his head and made a show of playfully smacking himself on the wrist.

On the issue of the mat having been placed actually *on* the step as opposed to the path before the step, opinions were divided. Again it came down to *Health & Safety* and *ease of access*, again difficult to gauge – unlike the issue of a lever being attached to the rear outside door when they'd been able to do a brief survey to gauge the effectiveness of the door closing with or without the lever. Because in this case it was only people stepping on and off the mat, it was less straightforward – as some were likely to step on and off the mat quicker than others.

Same with 'safety' – was the mat likely to be more visible on, or off, the step? If not clearly visible, what chance someone might go tripping over the mat and going hurtling into the pane of glass in the door, particularly at night.

When it came to the *shape* opinions were again divided. As Harold pointed out, a semi-circular mat did have a more convivial feel to it – particularly with its green and red interwoven pattern, whereas rectangular mats are inclined to be a little austere and less easy on the eye. Same with colours. Green and red were a bit traffic-lighty. Maybe a deep tan with a splash of green; or a bit of orange: orange being Marilyn's favourite colour. But whatever the colour, *shape* was the issue currently under discussion.

What was agreed was that the *shape* of the mat could be as important as the *placing* of the mat, which itself could be as vital as the *depth* of the mat.

How deep was the mat? Had anyone checked? Apparently not. Tom, who happened to have his tape-measure with him and Ken went to take a few quick measurements and report back, announcing that the mat was fractionally less than one inch in depth.

One inch in depth. An inch meant a significant raising of the foot, which was bound to affect stability.

'*Health & Safety*.'

'And *quick and ready* access,' added Tom.

'Depending on the angle you approach the mat from,' pointed out Harold.

'Or were left or right footed,' added Ken.

There were nods all round. It seemed they were finally getting somewhere.

That the depth of the mat was no less an issue than the shape and position of the mat, which itself bore direct links to the speed and direction of the approach and the age and circumstances of the person approaching.

At which point the meeting closed with a vote of thanks for attending from Marilyn and an assurance from Tom that the minutes would be forthcoming in the next day or two.

Back outside, Edna was a little confused as to what they'd decided; whether the mat should, or shouldn't, have been placed on (or off) the step.

Which immediately became more or less a redundant issue, as on leaving Marilyn's side of the building, it was noticed that the mat had disappeared, which – at first glance – barely seemed possible. How could a mat simply disappear off a step during the course of a meeting? They contemplated a return to Marilyn's flat, but instead Harold agreed to ring Marilyn once back in his flat, to put her in the picture: that, during the course of the meeting, the mat had mysteriously disappeared from the step.

The question was: who could have removed the mat from the step? It was difficult to say. And with the mat having disappeared there was now nothing to wipe your feet on *before* entering the building.

They were back to their side, each taking care not to trip over the step and to wipe their feet on a mat they all noticed had suddenly appeared *inside* the building – as in, actually *in* the hallway once through the door. It was smaller and a little thinner than the other mat, a deep-sea blue in colour. The question was: who could have placed the mat inside the door whilst they'd been at a meeting next door? Harold agreed to put Marilyn in the picture, that in addition to the mat disappearing from in front of the door – another mat had mysteriously appeared behind the door.

'If it isn't one thing, it's another,' said Tom.

Recollections From
A Hospital Bed

Like some Heath Robinson contraption a metal crane reaches over my head with a pulley on the end to poke my leg in the air to make an angle of about sixty degrees. A fair proportion of me is encased in white bandaging, including my head. And my mouth is caged.

I have a choice of three positions – I can look left, look right or up at the ceiling. I don't like to look at the ceiling for too long as the fluorescent light burns like a silver flare behind my eyes. I am hurting enough elsewhere. My preferred option, though not the most comfortable, is looking left where there is a small window set in the wall. The window has a slightly oval frame like a ship's port-hole. From my position at the end of the line and with my head resting on the pillow I can just about see an oval of greyish white sky through it. Sometimes I just lie and stare at the sky. Then I change to one of the other positions.

It's a bit like a theatre: the spotlights are above, hooked to the ceiling. A line of ten beds on the far side and a line of ten beds on this side provide the setting. Each bed has a number above the head-rail written in black paint. *One* is the first bed on the opposite side, ending in *Twenty* above the bed at the end of my row. I am number *Eleven*. Nearly every bed is occupied. I occasionally look at the line of heads in the beds opposite, most of which lilt or waver from side to side in states of semi-slumber. 'Time' is one commodity not in short supply here.

Green-smocked nurses and orderlies hover in the wings ready to make their make their entry – bursting onto the scene brandishing instruments and bottles and kidney-shaped containers.

To my right is Bed *Twelve*. Bed *Twelve* is Dennis who likes to have a laugh and look on the bright side because it helps everyone get through the day. They prop him up against the back rail and he just sits back and chuckles at the various comings and goings. 'What can you do of you can't have a laugh?' he'd say to anyone he thinks is listening, which in his book is most people. When the nurse comes to give him his tablet and medicine he's ready and waiting...

'Here she is...here she is. Come to poison me.' He has a gruff voice and looks gruff – big round face and spiky hair – ex-army.

'You drink it, I'll drink it,' he says, looking round to check we're on his wavelength. No-one's listening. Some are reading a paper or trying to sleep. The nurse denies everything as she wheels her trolley away. Dennis sits back and chuckles after her.

'You drive carefully now, no running anyone over.' He follows her movements. 'Women drivers!' He chuckles and sips his tea.

I can't say much because of the wires round my mouth. A nurse approaches.

'Come to take your blood-pressure,' she says reaching for my arm to wrap it in a belt a bit like a big fat bum-belt. I like the feel of it inflating; the tightness on my arm, like it's cutting off the blood. She sticks a thermometer under my tongue and turns to her trolley. I'm tempted to brace my teeth against it to see if it will crack, but I don't. She pops the thing back on the trolley and turns to leave.

'Okay?' I manage to utter.

She turns looking a little puzzled and nods. Then turns again and wheels the trolley back to the end of the ward.

Mornings drift into afternoons without anyone really noticing. The only sounds – muffled voices from somewhere off-stage and the squeak of rubber soles on polished linoleum. There are light snores from the beds opposite. I decide to change my position, turning to my left. My eyes are drawn to the port-hole. By raising myself on my elbows I'm able to see a little more sky beyond the small circular window. I can see the corner of a building and the tops of one or two trees. I lever myself a little higher and can see the sky has darkened and there seems to be a bit of mist drifting its way in from the city. It soon gets to be uncomfortable leaning on my elbows, so I ease my way down again and settle in my lying position, staring at the ceiling. I have a headache and it seems to be getting worse.

I change my position to the right. Dennis is snoring. I see a figure approaching. It's a doctor – small, dapper-looking Asian guy complete with collar, suit, tie; neat, orderly, business-like. He speaks in a business-like way, looking at me and then at his notes, flicking through the papers clipped to the board. Maybe he realises talking is difficult and that I can only manage mumbling sounds.

'Hello,' he says, holding out his hand. I shake his hand and mumble hello. He looks at his notes and then looks at me.

'You have a number of injuries, some of which you may know about, some of which you may not. I'll run down the list.' He's still looking at me and I nod. He refers again to his notes.

'You have fractures in the right tibia and fibula and a hair-line fracture of the femur and some tearing of the thigh muscle on your left leg. Three of your ribs are broken. Your jaw is fractured and it's possible there may be some disturbance in the brain tissue in the right rear of the cerebral cavity. You've also ruptured your right patella tendon. How are you feeling?' I shrug.

'Can you remember what happened?'

I nod. I can remember a bit of what happened. 'Bike crash,' I just about manage to utter.

'Motorbike?'

'Cycle.'

He nods and looks at his paper. 'Well – your position is serious but not, at this stage, life-threatening. Do you require anything?' I shrug and point at the wire round my mouth.

'It's okay. I understand,' he says. 'Don't tire yourself by trying to talk. Just get plenty of rest. And drink plenty of water. Are you eating okay? Just nod or shake your head.'

I nod.

'Good.' He writes something on a sheet, turns and leaves.

It's time to look up again. I'm getting used to the lights now. They're still sharp but I find them easier on the eye. Recollections of the accident are vague. Apparently it wasn't so much the car hitting me as the car behind running over me that caused the problems. From that point on it's mostly blank.

I ease myself up to look again through the port-hole. I see that the sky has darkened by what appears to be a slowly encroaching mist. The corner of the building opposite has almost disappeared from sight. It aches being in this position for too long and hurts my hip, so I lie down and stare at the ceiling.

I see someone approach. Bed *Five*. Alan. He's been to the bog and is shuffling his way back stopping for a chat on the way. He's okay. He asks how things are going. I point to the wire round my mouth and mouth 'okay'. He nods and points to his foot and shrugs. He offers his newspaper. I shake my head but offer a word of *thanks* anyway. I raise a hand as he turns to go.

I am in the process of taking a sip of water from the beaker on my locker, which involves using a plastic straw. I'm drawing water through the straw when another figure approaches. This time it's Bed *Three*, Michael. Michael's always on his way to somewhere or on his way back from somewhere. He likes to talk. He stops at the end of my bed and says 'how's things?' I point at myself and at the wire frame round my mouth. He nods and glances to his left, placing a hand on the hand-rail at the end of the bed. He's in a bad way. He keeps looking left, keeping an eye out for his next audience or a nurse who might be about to come along and admonish him for talking about his habit. He also likes scratching his balls. He leans forward.

'My problem's the drink,' he says, pointing at himself and pausing a moment. He has a strong Irish accent and it's difficult to make out what he's saying.

'And when I say drink...I mean *drink*.' He glances to his left and totters a bit.

'Bottle of brandy – cider. A half pint of brandy here.' He points at a spot near the end of the bedrail.

'And a pint of cider here.' He points to a spot about four feet away at the other end of the rail. He holds his arms out to indicate the proximity of the two glasses, tottering a bit in the process. 'And when the half-pint glass is empty, it gets filled up again – to the top. Bottle a day!' He glances left and scratches his balls. 'I'm never without a drink – never! And, something else – when I go for a piss it's black – black as coal. That's what happens when you drink. Your piss turns black.' He stops and looks at the pulley-system holding my leg in the air.

'People tell me they like a drink. I'll tell 'em about liking a drink – going out for a drink, cos they don't know.'

He's becoming quite animated and leans forward glancing more furtively to his left. 'I'll drink half a pint of brandy before they've even lifted their glass – that's taking a drink. And – I'm epileptic. Do you know what that means, when you're an alcoholic...and epileptic?' He scratches his balls. I shake my head; it's difficult to imagine.

'Medication! I'll tell you about medication. I'm on more medication than a fucking chemist.' He looks to his right. 'I've had more tablets, more drugs, more fucking everything shoved into me than a fucking junkie.'

He leans further forward as if about to share a secret worth hearing, curling a finger to beckon me closer.

'You know the nurse with the short black hair – nice looking girl. I said to her 'I'll take you out for a drink darling. I'll take you out for a drink. I'll show you a night's drinking.'

He chuckles to himself. 'I'll show you what a night's drinking is.' He looks to his right. A nurse suddenly appears pushing a trolley. He flinches and bids a hasty retreat – vague notions of standing to attention.

'Come on Michael, time for your blood test,' she announces from some distance and with limited patience. He looks at me and chuckles.

'I told 'em,' he says, shuffling his way towards her. 'I told 'em. You might as well stick the fucking needle in a fucking brandy bottle.'

And with a turn of his head and a quick scratch of his balls, he's gone. I'm quite glad when he goes. Though he's in a bad way and it isn't necessarily his fault he makes my headache worse.

Again unnoticed, evening slips into night. Lights are lowered, vague shapes stir in the beds opposite. Sleep is difficult and I switch between bouts of semi-sleep and a dull pain running up the back of my neck.

There is a sudden commotion at Bed *Eight*. A screen has been pulled round a tall metal affair on wheels. Moments later, the screen is thrown back and following a number of disconnections, the bed is wheeled away. No-one appears to have noticed Bed Eight. And no-one appears to notice him being wheeled away.

I watch the entourage to the end of the aisle and then reach to my locker. By sitting up I can poke the straw through the cage to my lips and hold it there long enough to drink. My head is starting to throb; the pain is growing. I position myself to my left. The port-hole window is only partly visible. I raise myself for a last glance beyond it, but there isn't much to see at such a late hour, particularly as the mist has now thickened to an all-encompassing fog.

I abandon the scene beyond the window and lie back to face the ceiling. I feel weariness beginning to take over. And then – as if by magic – I close my eyes.

How To Read The Opening Of 'The Iron Man' By Ted Hughes [In 2008 AD]

Two lines awaited – one on the left of the door, one on the right, as the teacher strode with a confident air through the door to the front of the class and threw a switch to throw a rectangle of light onto a white screen to the right of the centre of the front wall.

That done, she placed four documents on the front of the desk and returned to the door to indicate the children should enter the room single-file and take their places behind their tables placing their bags to the side of the tables to await invitation to take their seats.

On completion of the ritual infant-style greeting, they were invited to take their seats, have their pencil-cases on the desk ready, and to sit up face the front and listen...

When she could be reasonably sure all were facing the front and listening, the teacher looked to her right and extended a three-foot stick in the direction of five lines of writing within the rectangle of light, each on a new line numbered one to five, and highlighted by bullet-point markers.

She then spoke to the class. What she said was...

'These are our *Objectives* for today's lesson. There are five *Objectives*. Does everybody understand there are five *Objectives* for today's lesson?' Everyone appeared to understand that there were five *Objectives*.

'These...' She returned to the screen wiggling the stick a little more animatedly. 'Are the things you'll learn in this lesson. That is to say: things that when you came into the room, ie. now…you likely didn't know, or don't know, whereas when you leave the room, ie at the end of the lesson – you will know. Do you understand what is going to happen…in terms of what you *don't* know, as opposed to what you *will* know…in the course of this lesson?'

All indications were that they understood that what they didn't know was – during the course of the lesson – likely to be replaced by what they would know.

Good. With 'Introduction To Lesson' successfully behind them and ticked in her lesson-plan: everyone seeming to understand what was expected of them during the course of the lesson, they were in a position to move on.

What would be expected of them would be to acknowledge each *Objective*…in the order it was 'met', indicated by the teacher pointing the stick at the screen on the right-hand side at various stages of the lesson.

With the *Objectives* written in their books it was time for the overhead projector to leap into action, displaying, amongst other things, the title of the book they were about to read: 'The Iron Man' by Ted Hughes – followed by a short introduction of fifty-one words set out in five and a half lines. Would anyone like to read the introduction aloud? Hands indicated a number of people would like to read the introduction aloud. Penelope Davers read the introduction, after which the teacher waggled the stick in the direction of the white-board. Did anyone know *why* the teacher was wiggling the stick at the white-board? John Holdsworth knew why. Because they'd met the first *Objective* of the lesson – *Learn at least three facts about the author*…ie. something they didn't know when they came in the room, but would know when they left it. The teacher commended him and drew a tick next to the line in her lesson-plan and instructed the pupils (or 'learners' as the education 'experts' had deemed they should be labelled) to put a tick next to the *Objective* they'd written in their books.

Next they looked at the paragraph they were going to read underneath the introduction. It was an extract from 'The Iron Man'. Could everyone see the extract from where they were sitting? Everyone could see the extract quite clearly. They were going to read the lines of writing collectively, that is...reading it together. It was on completion of the reading that the stick was again seen pointing in the direction of the screen. Why was the stick pointing at the screen? Ashmal Rashid knew why. Because they'd met the second *Objective! To infer understanding of a text by reading it with appropriate intonation and feeling*...Did everyone understand that the *Objective* had been met? Everyone understood the *Objective* had been met, so once the teacher had ticked the next line of her lesson-plan and the pupils had ticked the *Objective* in their books, they were in a position to move on.

Back to the eight lines of writing.

Now – how many sentences were in the lines of writing? They counted them. There were six sentences. Good. Who can find the longest sentence, and prove they'd found it by reading it aloud? Frowns were followed by the raising of hands – about eleven in all. About half the class had found the longest sentence.

'Who'd like to read the longest sentence?' There were fifteen volunteers to read the longest sentence. Quite a number, it seemed, wanted to read the longest sentence to the rest of the class.

Heather Bakersfield it was who read the sentence, reading directly from the screen. She read it well, without tripping up over any of the words and, following a lead from the teacher, was awarded a round of applause.

They were still applauding as the teacher waved the stick in the direction of the third *Objective*: which had just been met: *Identifying an 'extended' sentence in a paragraph of writing and reading it with appropriate intonation.* The teacher ticked her plan, the children ticked their boxes and the lesson moved on.

Back to the opening of 'The Iron Man' by Ted Hughes. How many words were in the longest sentence? Fingers pointed in the direction of the screen. Kenneth Baker though he had the answer; twenty-three. But a chorus of shouts told him he was wrong – he'd miscounted. Jennifer Squires gave the answer – twenty-four. And she was right. The longest sentence in this piece of writing had twenty-four words.

Being a clever teacher, she had deliberately avoided using the word for a collection of lines in a piece of writing, which was....*Paragraph!* The word was chanted as the stick was pointed at the spelling on the screen. What had they just done? Maria Ijakowsky knew what they'd just done: *Identified and established – in context – the meaning and spelling of the word for a collection of sentences with a unity of purpose!*

The teacher ticked her lesson-plan, the children ticked their boxes and were ready to press on with their reading of the opening to 'The Iron Man' by Ted Hughes.

Back to Ted Hughes's...*paragraph.*

Now...Ted Hughes has used an 'extended' sentence, which might be...?

'*Compound* or *Complex* came the cry...which was correct, Ted Hughes could, conceivably have used either in the opening to his story. The stick waggled at a display pinned to the wall above the screen...

'*Compound*'...*two independent clauses joined by a co-ordinator.* '*Complex*'...*an independent clause joined by one or more dependent clauses by use of a subordinator...*' Can everyone see how Ted Hughes opted to use independent clauses joined by a co-ordinator and/or an independent clause joined by one or more dependent clauses by use of a subordinator in the opening to his story? Hands went up (or *some* hands went up). Some, at least could see what Ted Hughes had set out to do in the opening to his story.

Now...back to the paragraph. Most of the sentences are...

'*Simple*' sentences – good. In that they convey *one* simple, single idea...

Now...The teacher waggled her stick and turned to the paragraph on the screen. The thing is...Can some of Ted Hughes's *simple* sentences be changed into *extended* sentences by rearrangement of clauses and/or employment of *conjunctions* or alternative *connectives* that might be deemed appropriate?

A good question: one that only time and a forest of scratched heads would, at some point later in the lesson be able to answer. When the answer came, it was a resounding 'yes': they *had* been able to rearrange some of Ted Hughes's sentences by employment of *conjunctions* or alternative *connectives*... which following a lead from the teacher was greeted by a round of applause from all sides of the room and a firm ticking of *Objective Five...Construction of compound and/or complex sentences by rearrangement of clauses and/or employment of conjunctions or alternative connectives!*

After which – and bang on time – the stick was waved once again in the direction of the screen. With all today's *Objectives* well and truly ticked there was just one question (Objective!) remaining. Which was....

What happens in the opening to 'The Iron Man' by Ted Hughes?

The teacher scanned lines of blank expressions. She sensed they needed prodding; they often needed prodding toward the end of the lesson.

Katherine Maypole had the answer. She knew what happens in the opening to 'The Iron Man' by Ted Hughes...*An arrangement of simple and complex/compound sentences formed by subordinators and other appropriate connectives combine in a unity of purpose* is what happens. Which, of course, was absolutely correct! The evidence was right there, set out in clear easy-to-follow *Objectives* sitting on a projector-screen – signed, sealed and delivered by the teacher who ticked the last of the lines on her plan and having instructed the class to follow suit, had them pack their things away and stand in silence behind their tables.

Did everyone understand that the *Objectives* of the day's lesson had been met, in full? Hands hit the air. Everyone, it seemed, had grasped the fact that the *Objectives* of the day's lesson had been met. Good.

'Give yourselves a round of applause,' said the teacher, almost managing a smile. Well done class – well done teacher! Well done everyone.

*Education...Education...Education...*came the cry, almost in a single voice and reaching just about every corner of the room.

⋘

The Issue Of A Repair To A Hole In A South London Road

Almost on the dot of seven am. two men – employees of the *Highways Maintenance Incident Response* Team – clad in luminous yellow tops, emerged from an open backed wagon and made their way briskly alongside a stretch of road in Blackheath, South East London to begin their daily contribution in the never-ending battle to keep the city moving. One carried what appeared to be a lab-top in one hand and at an appropriate moment stopped at the roadside and tapped a number of digits into the screen. On a grim, drizzly morning such as this, the company's claim emblazoned on the side of the wagon that they 'get their job done in order to let us get our jobs done' would likely go more unnoticed than was intended, but it was there all the same, and to be fair, not without some justification. On this – the second of their eight kilometres a day hike in the wagon – they had made a discovery that might add a little more weight to the claim, if only temporarily.

A pot-hole on Shooters Hill Road. Given the shortage of funds to resurface the roads every year, the team were reduced to tackling each issue as and when it arose as best they could. Which, in practice, meant that within twenty-four hours of them arriving on the scene another member, or members, of the 'Response Team' would appear to complete the job; ie. make it safe – in effect, complete the resurfacing and limit the likelihood of it causing long-term interruption to the flow of traffic.

But for now it was down to Alec and Indragura, an ex-Gurka – to get the wheels in motion by laying six cones, effectively marking a rectangle around the offending portion of road. Being seasoned campaigners they were capable of doing twenty or thirty pot-holes a day, more if necessary – some achievement, not helped by the fact that most of the roads in these parts are built on old roads, very old roads in some cases – Roman and such like.

The pot-hole that had appeared in this particular stretch of road was roughly speaking four feet wide and five feet long though it was difficult to be precise.

First task was to dump the 'mix' on top of the hole. Their job being to spread the mix…a thick black tar-like concoction into place, using a spade and trying to complete the task in such a way the people wouldn't even know they'd been there. A couple of minutes were often all it took to fill the hole with the mix and bash it into place with a spade.

This pot-hole was a relatively easy one to fix. Once filled with the thick black tar-like stuff the next job was to pat it down, then – in the blink of an eye – pack up and get back to the wagon to check the details for the next job remained as scheduled.

Having patted the top of the pile, they were in the process of turning to pick up the signs and the cones to get back to their wagon, when they were distracted by a voice, and on turning, found the owner of the voice – a middle-aged to elderly woman wearing glasses and a long coat and carrying a plastic bag stood behind them looking down at the road.

The woman was giving both road and Alec and his colleague Indragura-the-Gurka, a thorough viewing, all indications being that she was about to come out with some observation about what they'd been doing. Moments later she mouthed her observation, directing her comment at Alec.

'I have to say – I could do better than that.'

Alec looked down and then looked at his spade.

'Than what?'

'Than what you've just done – filling in that hole in the road.'

Alec gave the repair-job another look, and his spade.

'It's only temporary,' he said, looking in the direction of the woman.

'Well I could still do better than that,' she said, looking both at the spade and the mound of tar. Alec looked back into the road.

'We could whack it again if you like. Give it a few more whacks,' he said.

The woman thought about it for a moment.

'Let me put it this way. If that was your drive and you'd paid someone a large sum of money to come and fix the hole in your drive and they'd said `okay guv. That'll be two hundred quid.` What would you say?'

Alec looked at the lump.

'I'd say it's not a permanent repair. It's a temporary repair. The hole in your drive would likely be a permanent repair. The 'Incident Response Team' will be along within twenty-four hours to make this a permanent repair.' The woman looked up and then across at Indragura-the-Gurka, perhaps trying to figure out the extent of his involvement or maybe what nationality he was.

'That's rubbish,' said the woman, nodding at the road and taking a few steps towards it. Alec was watching her, moments later stepping closer, taking advantage of a moment's reprieve.

'I understand what you're saying,' he said, giving the lump another look just to confirm both their points. 'But like I say, I could give it a few more taps. A few more whacks with the spade.'

'A few more whacks?' asked the woman. 'How many?'

Alec looked down at the road and at the spade.

'Dunno,' he said. It was difficult to say how long they could hang around whacking the repair into shape when they'd likely got other jobs waiting for them at the end of the line back in the wagon. The woman turned on the spot, a half-raised bag indicating the point she was trying to make.

'I mean, it isn't very technical is it? It's like icing a cake. You put the base on the table then you put the second base on top, then you stamp it down a bit, then you put the icing on top, then you smooth it all....flat,' she said, levelling her bag at waist height and easing it back and forth like she was levelling out the air between them.

'Yes. I understand what you're saying,' said Alec, turning to the woman. 'But like I say, I could give it a few more taps, a few more whacks. It's not a permanent repair you see. It's a temporary repair.'

'So is that why it's sticking up in a hill?' the woman asked. Alec looked down.

'But it's still safe,' he said. 'Temporary, but safe.'

She looked across at Indragura-the-Gurka who had been contemplating putting the stuff back in the wagon, but was now waiting a moment in case the instruction came to give the road a few more whacks with the spade.

'I suppose you could give it a few more whacks,' said the woman.

Alec might have been on the verge of springing back into action there and then if another wagon hadn't pulled up behind them – all eyes, including the woman's, turning to see who it was.

It was a similar wagon to theirs, but larger. Another white van with *London – You're going places – and we're right behind you...*written in jagged letters on its side. Inside the wagon two figures in larger luminous jackets and longer coats reached across, opened the doors and launched themselves onto the side of the road. Both wore service trousers and carried what appeared to be weather-protected lab-top type screens.

All continued to watch the two men approach, both wearing hard-hats, one nudging the hat to run his eye over the scene, taking in the repair-job just done to the road. Curt greetings followed as one of the men drew the lab-top like appliance to his waist and appeared to scroll something on a key-pad. His colleague continued to eye the heap in the road and pulled his jacket tighter. He hated this fucking weather. He had long since decided his next posting would be fixing the roads in Los Angeles.

'Finished?' he asked, cocking an eye at the lump of tar and pocketing a pencil in the top of his jacket. Alec half answered and half looked across at the woman standing close by, the plastic bag still clutched tightly in one hand.

'Not happy,' he said, indicating it was the woman who wasn't happy. The woman looked again at the pile of tar on the road, as did the other man from the second wagon, drawing closer to inspect the job from a different angle.

'Not happy madam?' said the first man, the question falling halfway between a statement and a question.

The woman cast her eye across all the men, including Indragura-the-Gurka, and returned it to the pile of tar on the surface of the road.

'Well – as I just said to your friends…If that was your drive and you'd paid someone a large sum of money to come and fix a hole in your drive and they'd said `okay guv, I'll fix it but that'd be two hundred quid` what would your friends say? You wouldn't be happy.'

The first of the men from the second wagon looked to investigate the woman's point a little more closely. Seconds later, his colleague joined her – venturing a foot, nudging the perimeter of the pile. The first man was back to the pavement and releasing the catch on his lab-top.

'The thing is…' he said, tapping a key and looking first at the screen and then at his watch. 'It's only temporary. The 'Incident Response' boys will be along soon to make it permanent.'

'So till then it stops like this,' said the woman, swapping the bag from one hand to the other to give her shoulder a moment's respite.

Three men looked down. Indragura-the-Gurka was staying out of it. It was all part of a day's work to him.

'Till then yes,' the man said, looking down to see his screen burst into life with a proposition that with luck would seem to serve both parties' interests for the time being at least.

'What I'll do is this…' He'd acquired a useful knack of being able to tap into his lab-top and hold a conversation at the same time.

'What it is…we are___' He indicated himself and his colleague who had returned from the pile of tar to the front of the wagon. '*Highways Maintenance – Inspection Division.* It's our job to keep an overall view on things, like a bird's eye view of everything that's going on in the department. So..' He tapped again and scrolled back to the previous line. 'What I'm going to do is this.' The cursor came to a halt. 'I'm going to record your complaint okay. And I'm going to send your complaint to our Head-Office and what'll happen is….'

The woman watched him tapping into the screen and his colleague closing in to witness the fact that he was undertaking the appropriate procedure given a complaint had been made. To make *her* point clear, the point she'd made only minutes earlier to Alec and Indragura-the-Gurka, she approached the second inspector.

'What I mean is. Like I told your friends, it's like icing a cake. When you put the base down and put the icing on top you smooth it all flat.' She levelled a hand, easing it back and forth in the air. The man nodded and his colleague, the second inspector, moved round to give the mound another quick tap with his foot.

'Temporary though you see,' he said, stepping away from the repair and looking along the stretch of road.

'Well,' the woman said.

The first inspector had moved across and was giving the lump another viewing and then a quick kick, seeing things from the woman's angle, which was what they were encouraged to do – to see things not just from the department's point of view but from the point of view of anyone who might be affected by the work they were undertaking.

'We'll give it a few whacks, see what happens.' He had his eye on the other inspector. Being seen as attempting to address an issue raised by a member of the public there and then would likely count in their favour somewhere along the line. Plus – maybe the woman had a point. Maybe it was sticking up a bit more than it needed to.

Spade in hand and stepping out into the road under the watchful eye of everyone present, Alec gave four or five resounding whacks on the pile of tar. All eyes were on him and the pile. Indragura-the-Gurka, though not directly involved, was watching too and chuckling to himself. This was all part of being in England. England was like this. He liked working on the street and he liked the people. And England – he'd long since decided – was a good place to bring up his kids.

The men had gathered round to have a look at the effect of giving the mound a few quick whacks with the spade. The first inspector had a pen and moved to the side where the woman was, by this stage, little more than an idle bystander.

'What we'll do is – I'll take your name. And your comments will be recorded at Head Office and I expect you'll receive a formal reply, probably within ten working days.' He took the pen and turned to the woman. 'But what it is – I need to confirm you're happy with that.'

The woman did a quick tot-up. It wouldn't appear to be a problem. But she didn't want to make a lot of trouble. She didn't want to get the men sacked or anything like that. In some ways what she was saying was more a passing observation than a complaint. The inspectors were quick to reassure her. There would be no question of sackings or disciplining employees of the company. It was simply part of 'getting our job done in order to let you get your job done.' A public-relations side of the business that meant addressing issues that arose and following them up in what is seen to be an appropriate manner.

He scrolled through two pages and turned to his colleague who was tapping the pile of tar a few more times with his foot now that a few more whacks had been administered with the spade. He was back to his lab-top.

'Now, if I could have a few details.'

The woman filled him in on *name*, *address* and *circumstances*; ie. the course of events that led to her making the complaint, ie. spotting what was perceived to be a flaw in the work being undertaken whilst on her way from doing a bit of early-morning shopping – seeing the repair in the road that the men had just finished which was sticking up a bit and, to be frank, looked a bit of a mess.

The point was noted along with the time, date and the post-code. The next move was to get a few details of the job itself which would involve taking a few measurements and noting the time of undertaking and completing the work. He stepped across to have a quick word with his colleague.

Alec had finished whacking the mound with his spade. He called the woman, whose name was confirmed as Eileen Bladder, to come over a give her opinion. Indragura-the-Gurka stepped across too to have a quick look and a quick word with the first inspector.

There had possibly been a slight flattening of the surface of the pile but it still protruded some way from the surface of the road. The inspector joined them and knelt to measure the dimensions of the mound and its distance from the road surface.

Indragura-the-Gurka, finding himself next to Eileen, felt obliged to make an attempt at conversation. His English wasn't brilliant but it wasn't too bad. And he suspected striking up conversations with members of the public who were in the process of logging an official complaint might be seen as part of the job. Which he would have no argument with. He nodded in the direction of the men completing the measurements in the road.

'Not too long. Just need to measure the details of the hole,' he said stuttering over only one or two words.

Eileen Bladder looked up. She was still pondering the man's nationality, Maybe Egyptian or Indian, she didn't like to ask in case it came across as being rude.

'It isn't easy to get the tar in the hole to fit exactly right,' Indragura added, indicating the difficulty in getting these things right by folding the palms of his hands inwards and then outwards.

For the first time she looked him in the eye.

'You like working on the roads?' Each word was delivered slowly and with sufficient clarity to ensure he understood the question. He nodded – indication he most probably had understood, if not entirely, sufficient to have her put a few more questions without risk of causing offence. She put her bag on the floor and looked up.

'And you are...?' She hesitated, confident enough after their introductions to pursue a few of the man's circumstances if a trifle unsure about the answer she was seeking. No way a problem as far as Indragura was concerned. This was one of the things he liked about being in England, opportunities to strike up impromptu conversations with members of the public.

'I used to be a Gurka – or am *still* a Gurka,' he said, smiling at being in a position to establish his credentials more precisely. The claim had Eileen intrigued. He was watching the pile of tar.

'I was in the British army for twenty years.'

Eileen was watching the pile with him. Her knowledge of armies was sketchy, her knowledge of the Gurkas' contribution to these things sketchier still. She thrust a chin and swapped the plastic bag from one hand to the other. Indragura was happy enough with the way things were turning out. He liked talking to people. If asked what he liked about his job, he'd likely to say 'the people.' That was why he'd come to London, because he liked London, and he liked the job.

'Twenty years,' he said. 'In the British army.' He looked to the middle of the road. Eileen looked too.

'That's a long time,' she said. 'A long time to be in the army.'

Indragura grinned. It was a helluva long time. For a second he seemed on the verge of laughing which maybe prompted

Eileen to put another question. 'So you've been around a bit then, when you were in the army.'

Indragura looked down the road, looked up the road, and laughed. He'd been around all right – which was one of the reasons he was happy to settle down in England.

'Yeh...I been around.' He drew his arms in two arcs. 'I been all over – India, Syria, North Africa, Italy.'

Eileen watched the first inspector approach. He was keying a few more points into his keyboard. He looked up when close enough to update Eileen on the situation.

'Okay madam. What it is...I've recorded the details on the computer – that's your details, the time of your arrival on the scene and a brief description of the job that employees of the company undertook – a temporary measure to deal with the flaw in the road surface, which – in the member of the public's opinion – was inadequately done, and that striking the resurfaced area repeatedly with a spade was also deemed to be inadequate. You saw the men striking the surface of the road with a spade, is that correct?'

Eileen Bladder was looking from man to road and back again. And eyeing the lab-top. All of which brought her back to the fact that she didn't want to get anyone into trouble.

'Don't worry, it's not a question of getting people into trouble,' said the inspector, still tapping and checking the results popping on and off the screen, seeking to catch Indragura-the-Gurka's eye as confirmation that members-of-the-public making representations regarding work undertaken by the company could, in no way, be construed as 'making trouble'.

Leaning on his spade, Indragura-the-Gurka grinned. He and the inspector were as close to strangers as was Eileen, but there was something about occasions such as this that was all part of being in England: something 'official' happening that made you feel you were a part of the action, if only from a distance: part of it yet in some ways not part of it – which suited him fine. The inspector was looking at his watch, reminding himself this was intended to be little more than a stop-off en-route to their next appointment in Eltham.

'Now – about how many times would you say the temporary repair was struck by the spade?' The inspector had the pen-like digit levelled above the screen, hopeful of getting a straightforward answer to what was essentially a straightforward question.

Eileen shrugged and for a moment her shoulders dropped. There'd been a few whacks at it. First with them all watching then when they weren't all watching.

'Don't know,' she said, still not convinced that whatever answer she came up with wouldn't in some way lead to sackings somewhere along the line, and in any case, struggling to recall the moment in detail.

'Okay. Don't worry. It's not a problem.' The inspector tapped a few more keys and looked up. 'What it is...I'm going to give you some options. You tell me which answer you think is the closest in terms of how many the times the repair was struck by the spade.' He scrolled again. 'Okay?'

Eileen was wondering why he pre-empted half the things he said with 'what it is...' when she was going to find out what it was when he told her.

'Okay.' It was the inspector speaking and still fiddling with his digits. 'Okay. What it is...' He made a point of reading directly from the screen – evidence the options were coming from the screen, ie. from the company, and not simply dreamed up on the back of a fag-packet.

'Two...six...ten. If likely more than ten, fifteen...twenty... more than twenty?'

Eileen tried remembering the options. And decided to take a stab at 'ten'.

'Well... probably about ten,' she said, though still far from sure about it – or the implications of committing herself either way.

'No worries,' said the inspector, tapping that section on the screen and scrolling it from top to bottom. 'It's just better if we can put a number. Makes it seem like we're more on-top of our game if you know what I mean.'

Indragura was chuckling and leaning on his spade. He nodded in the direction of the inspector.

'Busy man,' he said. Eileen would concede as much. They both continued to view the scene until Eileen stepped back. She was wondering, given that the man – Indragura – had done quite a bit of travelling, why he'd come to England. It was the easiest question he'd had put to him in a while.

'I like England,' he said, leaning more heavily on his spade. 'I like the people.' Eileen felt temporarily uplifted, taking it she could include herself in his appraisal seeing as she was the one he was talking to.

'What's your name?' she asked, sufficiently buoyed to put the question and immediately wondering if she'd done the right thing in case they weren't supposed to disclose their names to members of the public. It wasn't an issue as far as Indragura-the-Gurka was concerned. He told her his name and grinned. He liked disclosing his name, it had a ring to it, particularly when you said it to people here in England.

Eileen wouldn't try repeating it for fear of getting it wrong.

The inspector was back, stepping over a few patches of tar, the lab-top still cradled in his arm.

'Right,' he began, putting the pen-like gadget to one side and turning to Eileen.

'I've entered details of the repair, that – in the complainant's opinion – was inadequately undertaken. And that subsequent attempt to correct the perceived fault – approximately ten whacks with a spade' He manoeuvred the screen to face him more fully. 'Also failed to correct the fault.' Now, if you would just sign here.' He extended the pen and saw her hesitate, maybe not wanting to be seen as making too much of a fuss, or even worse – contribute to someone getting sacked.

'Do I have to sign it?' she asked, looking to Indragura for an answer. But he was staying out of it. He wasn't one for getting involved in what was happening on the company's computer screens. The inspector was quick to reassure her.

'No, you don't *have* to sign it.' What I'll do is...enter *signature of complainant voluntarily withheld.* Which immediately had Eileen thinking maybe it would be best to sign it, rather than voluntarily withholding it which made it sound like she had something to hide. She took the pen. The inspector watched her sign in the space on the screen, visibly happier that the procedure could now be said to have been completed in full.

'Okay, cool,' he said, taking the pen and dotting a few closing digits on the screen. Then closing the lid and turning to his colleague who'd abandoned the repair with a view to maybe making a move. A job at Eltham was in the pipeline, it was already approaching eight-o-clock which meant they could be well behind schedule if they didn't make a move soon.

Indragura turned to Eileen, nodding at the goings-on in the centre of the road.

'Almost done – for now,' he added, a reminder the boys from the 'Response Team' would soon be along soon to complete the job. It struck Eileen she and Indragura had something in common: both standing on the outside looking in, so to speak. Reason enough to spark up a bit more conversation.

'So, when you were travelling around a lot – when you were in the army...' she began. 'You must have seen a lot and done a lot of interesting things...' She looked to check he'd got the gist of what she was saying. Indragura chuckled; he'd been around a bit, that was for sure.

'Been all over – Syria, North Africa, Italy,' he said, laughing at the irony of discussing such far flung places on a grey drizzly morning on a South London road. Eileen had never been to any of those places.

I suppose you have to get used to a lot of different food when you go around all these places,' she said. Indragura laughed. She was right there. He could certainly tell a tale or two about some of the food he'd eaten.

'Yeh...I've certainly eaten some strange food.' Eileen pulled a face.

'Goats' testicles,' he said. 'I lived on goat's testicles for a month.' He laughed, trying to picture how many of the guys standing in the immediate vicinity could lay claim to having survived on goats' testicles for a month.

Eileen had never knowingly eaten goat's testicles, nor been offered them as far as she could recall. She was beginning to feel a bit of sympathy. It can't have been easy being a Gurka. And it can't have been easy being a soldier in the army. Indragura was enjoying himself. It was conversations like this: off-the-cuff conversations with members of the public – on such topics as surviving on a diet of goats' testicles – that made the job worthwhile.

The men were back. The first inspector had his lab-top open and was pacing his way towards Eileen Bladder.

'Okay madam, just to confirm. Your complaint and comments have been forwarded to *Highways Maintenance – Customer Services Department.* You'll likely be hearing from them within seven working days.' He scrolled the page and tapped a key.

Behind, Alec and Indragura were removing cones from their spots in the road and the second inspector was returning to the wagon, possibly needing to explain the delay in making their job in Eltham.

'Okay. Now just one last thing madam. What it is...' He was stalling a moment at the dialogue-box that had suddenly appeared under the page's title. 'A few questions on how effectively you feel your complaint has been dealt with, okay?' Eileen nodded, by this stage resigned to whatever was required to bring events to a speedy conclusion.

'On a scale of one to ten, how far would you say your complaint was satisfactorily dealt with?'

The question had caught her off-guard. 'One to ten?'

'One to ten,' confirmed the inspector, the pen-like digit poised above the screen. 'Where *one* is least effective and *ten* is most.' Eileen wanted to be seen giving it some thought; a score of *eight* seemed a safe enough option. The inspector tapped the score. Indragura, passing close by laden with traffic-cones was chuckling away to himself. Repairs to holes in roads, scores tapped into computer-screens – it was all part of being in England. He followed Alec to the wagon. Eileen was watching him from a distance as the inspector looked up.

'And – on a scale of *one* to *ten*, where *one* is 'not at all' and *ten* is 'very', how far would you say you were dealt with in a helpful and courteous manner?' Eileen gave another impression of giving it some thought before quickly opting for *ten*. There seemed little point in complicating proceedings at this point.

'Thankyou madam. Now...'

Alec, Indragura and the second inspector were packed and ready to go. Eileen had registered an *eight* on how far she would be likely to, or encourage others to, make a formal complaint to the company on future occasions – but with a reminder that it was only because the repair was sticking up in the first place and looking a bit of a mess that she'd stopped on her way home from shopping.

'I understand that madam. But what it is – the 'Incident Response' boys will be along within twenty-four hours to complete the job, ie. make it safe, make it like you'd never have known they'd been there.'

'Only temporary,' said the second inspector, joining his colleague. Eileen nodded. Indragura-The-Gurka was already back in the first wagon.

The inspector extended a hand which Eileen Bladder shook. Within seconds the men were back in their respective wagons and seconds after that, on their way to the next job in Eltham.

Eileen Bladder shuffled the plastic bag to give her carrying-hand a break and looked back at the mound sticking up from the surface of the road; a bit like a Christmas pudding it suddenly occurred to her, along with a parting thought that – despite what anyone said – left to her she'd have likely done a far better job than that.

[A thanks to the BBC documentary series 'The Route Master Running' June '13 which gave me the idea for the story and from which one or two lines of dialogue were taken.]

Margarita – Mark Two

[A sequel to 'Margarita' ... 'Call These Stories', where our hero was left picking up the pieces after bringing Margarita home only to have her – admittedly due to his own carelessness – slumped as lifeless (and useless) as an old inner tube over the arm of the chair!]

The first time had been a shame – about Margarita and the cigarette; burning a hole in her to have her slumped over the arm of the chair like that. But that was then, and this is now, and – as they say – there is no point in crying over spilt milk.

He'd actually given it a few days before taking her to the bin and setting off once again into town armed with his shoulder bag, his wallet, and on this occasion an intention to be there and back before it started to get really busy on the Tube and trains.

Town was the usual mix of people milling round looking flustered and the whirr of buses and taxes, especially in and around the main street with its union-jack shops and tee-shirts; but in many ways that's what you expect when you go to town: bustling and busy in a way that, for a while at least, makes you feel you want to be a part of it.

Unlike last time he now knew which streets to head down, finding the shop without too much trouble: same shop but a different woman serving him, this one a darker skinned woman smiling as she passed Margarita Mark-Two over the counter and took the money. She was already folded and conveniently parcelled in a polythene bag which seemed the best way to get her home, having her stay that way till they got back. Getting her out on The Tube would be a bit awkward if it was busy, and in any case, he knew about Margarita now – no need to read about her on the label. It was actually quite straightforward, you just had to be a bit careful. Unlike last time when it had all ended in tears – her tears – draped over the arm of the chair with a cigarette burn the size of a golf-ball in her thigh. It had all been very unfortunate, but he wouldn't be making the same mistake again. This time he'd be more careful, and a bit more considerate; maybe not even smoke a cigarette after their opening sex-session, or, if he couldn't help having one, make sure he held the cigarette well away from her, maybe in his other hand.

An hour or so later stepping from the bus it was back to the familiar schlep up the stairs, huffing and puffing their way to the top where, like before, he'd take a few moments searching for the keys in his pocket.

From then on it would hopefully be plain-sailing. A cup of tea first; he was a stickler for his cup of tea, as he suspected was Margarita Mark-Two if the last Margarita was anything to go by. And then, having sorted the preliminaries, a few moments together on the sofa; maybe pop a CD on as he set about putting her in the picture regarding the next few days. Tomorrow – a cup of coffee down the road and maybe a stroll in the park and then back for an early evening sex-session. Then, the day after, which was Sunday – a surprise appearance at the pub just outside Shrewsbury where his parents always went every Sunday for lunch after church – a big pub, with a garden and a play-area for the kids. He couldn't be certain they'd be there but he knew there was a fair chance, and even if they weren't it would be a day out, a nice train ride, see a bit of countryside for a few hours – maybe do them both a bit of good.

It seemed an ideal opportunity to put her in the picture regarding his parents...how he didn't get on with them too well, not having seen them for nearly two years and how he'd been a bit of a disappointment to them, not having married or 'given them any grandchildren' as they'd put it, or had a proper job or a nice house to live in with its own garden. How his father was quite rich and short-tempered and had a thing about people 'wasting their opportunities' and 'failing to make the most of their lives'. His mother being incredibly fussy and appalled when she'd come to visit him in his last flat which was small and only had two cooking rings. How it was her one and only visit and one visit too many as far as she was concerned. Her not liking the area either, commenting on how many 'non-whites' there were, as she termed them, rather than Blacks or Pakistanis. Or 'Coloureds' his father had piped-up from the seat opposite, which was another way of putting it.

Then, like last time, it occurred to him he'd been going on a bit and maybe boring Margarita, possibly turning her off him and make her think about leaving. But seeing her sitting there bolt upright and full of smiles, she certainly didn't seem to mind. Or at least nothing was said.

It was with tea some way behind them that he decided to make his move. After the last time, he felt he knew Margarita a little better, knowing to approach her a bit more casually, not lean towards her too eagerly when taking a seat next to her on the sofa and drawing her to him. To take a bit longer brushing a hand lightly against her cheek – on closer inspection just like the first Margarita's cheek – cool and smooth as a bar of soap. Picking his moment to lean over and search out the soft oval of her mouth, her fingers splayed and idle, evenly spaced. Then, that special moment – the initial unveiling of her breasts, perfectly formed like two freshly plopped blancmanges, almost the mirror-image of the first Margarita,

On this occasion things went very much according to plan – a final dispensing with clothes under cover of darkness – a little more fondling, a little more kissing before getting themselves into position using the full length of the sofa and after a little manoeuvring, entering her with minimum fuss or resistance. This time – unlike before and maybe with the benefit of experience – finding himself more adept at timing his thrusts – going over the top pretty much on-cue as opposed to half an hour before it!

With their opening sex-session behind them, a cigarette was most definitely on the agenda, on this occasion leaving Margarita to her own devices for a while as he made his way to the window and stepped out onto the balcony, a favourite spot where he would often stand last thing at night smoking a cigarette and observing the distant lights of the city, and closer to home – the lights of traffic approaching the roundabout, in what from this distance looked like lines of tiny torches, whilst taking regular glances over his shoulder to where Margarita continued to sit perched upright on the sofa – unlike last time, when all he'd spotted was a plastic mat slumped over its arm as flat as an old inner-tube!

He drew on the cigarette trying to recall whether there was a beer in the fridge. He could do with a beer after what had turned out to be another quite eventful day.

Next day was the chance to venture out and show her a little of the local area – a brisk walk through the park though on this occasion probably missing out on the coffee. They'd had a cup of tea with their breakfast so maybe the coffee could wait a while.

It was quite something to be seen walking down the street together arm-in-arm, and then later in the park – all eyes, not surprisingly, drawn to Margarita.

'What you got there?' came the cry from a few kids passing on bikes.

'Margarita,' he would reply with a smile and a quick wave in their direction.

He contemplated taking a seat on a bench but something he'd noticed on first leaving the flat, was that Margarita's legs were permanently rigid, likely making sitting on a park-bench a bit of an ordeal. Best to keep moving, make their way past the swings and people stopping in their tracks for a closer look, some of them drawing their children away to stop them getting too close.

It had been a pleasant morning with hopefully an equally pleasant afternoon and evening to come. If the sex-session that followed was anything to go by it would certainly be a day to remember!

When it came to their sex-sessions, they'd agreed to experiment a little to stop either of them getting bored (which can happen with some couples), an agreement to try varying their positions – one of which was Margarita taking her turn to 'go on top', which, from his point of view, was a definite turn-on, seeing *her* riding *him* as opposed to vice-versa, her lips pouting in that tight oval shape and coming out with a whole range of expletives, stirring the pair of them to even dizzier heights. He'd be needing a whole packet of cigarettes if sessions such as that were to become the norm!

It was a quite bedraggled and almost haggard-looking figure crossing the room some twenty minutes later for his post-coital smoke, Margarita reclining in the arm of the sofa and giving him a knowing look. 'The fun and games might be over for a while but don't you be coming near me with that thing,' she seemed to be saying, which, in light of past events, seemed like a reasonable enough request.

First step of the following day's journey was getting into town where he decided to get a cab; one of those big black ones that seem to be everywhere you look. It saved messing about catching The Tube even if it was a bit expensive. When he told the driver they were off to meet his mother and father the driver looked in his mirror and said he thought he'd seen everything but maybe he'd been wrong, which neither of them understood, but he knew the cab drivers in London were a funny lot who were apt to come out with things you didn't always understand.

As things transpired, there were few problems. The first train wasn't too busy and was quicker than he'd imagined it would be. There'd been a few odd looks when he and Margarita had clambered on board and he'd put her on the seat next to him, positioning her next to the window to enable her to see some of the countryside as he set about putting her in the picture regarding the afternoon's arrangements. A few passengers had turned away or even got out of their seats altogether to give them a bit of privacy which was a nice touch even it wasn't really necessary.

When the ticket-man arrived he showed him the two tickets, explaining how he'd put Margarita next to him to let her see a bit of the countryside and they were off to meet his parents. The guard didn't say much; he just shook his head and then moved on.

With the ticket bit sorted, he set about preparing her, as best he could, for the events to follow: explaining that she might have to be a bit patient with his mother and father, particularly with it being Sunday which was church day! Twice a day sometimes. He told her about when he was young, when they'd had to go to church because, as they'd put it – 'everyone needs something to believe in'; which he hadn't really understood then and still didn't. Warning her too that the surprise of their son appearing on the scene with a woman in-tow after all this time, might take a bit of getting used to. And not to be too put out if his mother – or both of them – seemed a little taken aback.

By now they had the carriage entirely to themselves which gave them plenty of extra space and meant he could slip an arm round Margarita and draw her a little closer, a little physical reassurance to add weight to what he'd been saying. He even had a bizarre thought of them having a sex-session right there in the middle of the empty carriage, but obviously there was no way they'd actually go ahead and do something like that. Apart from it not being the time or place, they might pull into a station or the guard might make his way back through the train and interrupt them which might take a bit of explaining.

At one station they had to change trains which was a bit of a fuss, having to go through the business of getting off one train and clambering aboard another, and finding two empty seats with one next to the window and showing his tickets again. But even the new carriage more or less cleared within minutes, most people acknowledging the fact that couples liked a bit of time to themselves, or maybe they were just on a short hop to the next stop.

Leaving the station to another round of admiring looks, they quickly found the cab-rank and as they were the only ones waiting for a cab they didn't have long to wait.

The cab driver, a young Asian man, must have been a fan of Sundays or maybe he'd just been to a wedding, for he was chuckling away to himself from the minute they'd got in the cab till the minute they arrived outside the pub, the one near the church with a garden a few miles away.

Having clambered out of the cab with Margarita he took a quick look round. The pub was on the other side of the road and the garden where his mother and father would likely be was in all probability behind it. With the weather being ideal for sitting outside the pub he was fairly sure they'd be there. Going for a drink after church seemed like a good idea with churches tending to be rather cold uncomfortable places as far as he could recall. Had it been chilly or raining he would have had to rethink his plans, for his parents might not have been in the garden if it had been raining, or even in the pub at all. But as it had turned out, everything pointed to it being a quite momentous afternoon! He too quite fancied a beer after the journey and might even join them in a bite to eat, not having eaten anything since breakfast.

With Margarita gripped firmly under one arm, he crossed the road and made his way up the path to the entrance. There was no need to actually go in the pub at this point. To get to the garden you could go round the side.

Eyes followed as he passed a few tables, stopping by the trellis entrance to have a quick word with Margarita, reminding her what he'd said about being a bit patient and needing to watch her p's and q's. Scanning the scene it didn't take long to spot his parents, sitting at a table on the far side near the swings.

The moment had finally arrived. Gathering Margarita and giving her cheesecloth top a quick brush down, he made his way between the tables, taking care not to have her feet send pints of beer flying in all directions. Walking in full view like that with Margarita gripped tightly under one arm made him feel quite proud, a bit like a father leading his daughter down the aisle to be married – all eyes turning in their direction as he led her past tables of mums and dads, grandpas and grannies…all out for a bite to eat and pleasant afternoon in the sun.

The looks on his parents' faces when he suddenly sprang from behind them, Margarita clasped under his right arm. The pair of them struck dumb and quite overwhelmed, almost to the point of tears – his father too. Which admittedly took him back a bit, though maybe on reflection it should have come as no great surprise. Having their son turn up out of the blue, arm-in-arm with his new ladyfriend was bound to be a bit of a shock to the system.

The introductions turned out to be a bit hard work – and a bit one-sided, neither of them seeming to know what to make of Margarita, who – for her part – was on her best behaviour from the start.

If anything it was all a bit frosty, which was a bit disappointing and seemed a bit unfair. You'd have thought Margarita would be their kind of woman: quiet, unassuming, no way over-demonstrative or given to drawing attention to herself. No 'unladylike' habits like uttering expletives (except during sex-sessions) which was something they couldn't abide in women. And in no way could she be described as ugly if that was to be seen as an issue…rosy cheeks full of freckles, nice big smile – just what his father liked to see in a woman. And (though he'd never dream of raising it as an issue) available for sex-sessions morn, noon or night: any place, any preference – any position you liked!

It was all a little strange. And a quite different kettle of fish from the kids playing on the swings who, on first spotting

Margarita, were over in their droves, abandoning their swings and slides to view her close-hand, some moving in really close and making a real fuss of her, even as their parents were moving in to grab them from the other side.

'What's she called?' they cried, reaching to touch her cheek and make a grab for her feet.

'Margarita,' he replied, with a smile, holding her at arm's length to let them get a closer look and if they wished, take her in their arms to pass round.

Some wanted to take her on the swings or on the slide with them, which was another nice touch though he thought it best to leave them with a promise of 'maybe next time.'

All in all, a mixed afternoon – a bit disappointing in some ways but Margarita hadn't seemed too put out by it which, in many respects was the main thing. The driver who took them back to the station was the driver who'd brought them – still grinning from ear to ear as he dropped them at the station's entrance where they were met by more admiring looks before making their way through the barriers onto the platform to take their place next to the timetables pinned to the wall.

He held her close. It had been quite an ordeal, for her especially, and yet she'd managed to smile her way through it without even a hint of a crossed word. How many women could lay claim to that on meeting their partner's parents for the first time, and in such trying circumstances?

On the train she nestled her head against his shoulder. Though not really one for conversation, had she opted to speak, a second sense told him what he'd likely be hearing. That it was okay; not to worry. That everything had, in fact, been fine, and – believe it or not – gone more or less according to plan.

He drew her closer, stealing a quick kiss and gazing into eyes that were suddenly wider than he'd ever imagined.

'See,' he said, stroking her arm and nodding at a steady stream of passengers abandoning their seats to award them a little well-earned privacy.

'There's not all bad in people!'

Margarita offered little by way of reply, but he knew she was listening – likely hanging on his every word. It was as he kissed her again that the train began to pull away from the platform.

Lightnin's Tale

There was once a man driving along an old country lane generally minding his own business and doing his best to keep an eye on the road – no easy task with the car leaping its way from one pot-hole to another. In fact, leaping around so much, he barely had time to see a small fat pig dart out from the bushes and run across the road right in front of where he was heading.

The choice was simple enough – either hit the pig or slam on the wheel, maybe run the risk of swerving off the road and go diving into the nearest ditch. Which was exactly what he did! One minute driving along minding his own business, the next – sitting in the middle of a ditch with a small black pig running off in the forest wearing the biggest grin you ever saw on any pig.

He never set eyes on the pig again, but its parting shot was to leave him with two choices, or maybe three – either get himself and the car out of the ditch or have the pair of them stay in the ditch – or get out of the car and leave it sitting in the ditch, which would have meant one helluva walk. Sittin' there thinking about which it was going to be, it was soon clear there was only going to be two choices. There was no way he was going to be getting out of that ditch with the car, which meant getting out without the car or staying right where he was, stuck inside the car.

Which was what he was puzzling over when the po-lice came on the scene.

He didn't hear or see the po-lice arrive or even know they was in the vicinity till he looked up to see a blue light flashing and hear doors slamming.

Next thing he knew he's sitting there looking up at not one but two burly po-lice officers, both looking him up and down, clicking their tongues and wanting to know what he was doing sitting there in his wagon with the wagon sitting in a ditch.

'What you doin' here boy?' the first po-liceman says, looking at the wagon and then staring down the road till he got an answer.

Lightnin' – which was the man's name – couldn't think what to say apart from to tell him that he didn't do nothing 'cept drive along the track minding his own business and next thing have to steer the car to avoid a small black pig running 'cross the road and then go diving into a ditch.

The po-liceman didn't say nothing; he just stepped round the car and said something to the other policeman who at first didn't say nothing either, just looked into the window checking the front and back and then turned to Lightnin'.

'You been drinking boy?' He spoke in his gruffest voice, whilst the other po-liceman was bending down and giving each of the wheels a closer inspection.

'No sir I ain't drunk. I ain't one for taking a drink when I know I'm going to be driving my car along the road,' says Lightnin' shaking his head like he wanted it to be known he meant what he was saying. So the same po-liceman looked down the road again, turned and spat on the road and shifted his hat. The other po-liceman had come round from examining the front wheels and was looking through the rear window.

'So if you ain't drunk how comes you sittin' there in the ditch?' A simple enough question even if it seemed like he hadn't been listenin' to a word Lightnin' had been tellin' him, or maybe just not hearing the bits he didn't want to be hearing.

So he told them again about driving along the road minding his own business when a little black pig come running 'cross the road and how he had a choice. He could either hit the pig or he could go swerving off the road and go diving in the nearest ditch, which was what he done and was why they were looking down and seeing him sitting there behind the wheel in the middle of a ditch.

The second po-liceman – the meanest-looking of the two spat on the ground and looked the length of the wagon.

'So you tryin' to tell me you gone driving in the ditch because you give right of way to a little fat pig when it was running 'cross the track?'

Lightnin' took a moment to think about what the po-liceman was saying, 'cause though that was kind o' what happened, it didn't sound quite right the way he was saying it and all Lightnin' could think was he done the best he could. He din't mean anyone no harm, not even the pig running out in front of him which was why he'd gone swerving off the road and gone diving in the ditch.

But the po-liceman, who was no fool, took out a little black book and started writing stuff in it and Lightnin' could guess what he was writing was about him driving the car off the road and into the ditch. When he finished writing he looked both ways up and down the track and then turned to Lightnin' slipping the book back in his pocket.

'Okay boy, you gonna have to come with us. You gone and put your wagon in a ditch and that's against the law in this county, and on this particular stretch of road.'

So Lightnin' couldn't see any way out of the situation other than to get out of the car and do what the po-liceman said, telling 'em he done the best he could and din't mean no-one any harm.

But the po-lice din't seem too interested in whether he was doing anyone any harm. All they was interested in was getting Lightnin' into town and getting their name next to his on the crime-sheet which would be sufficient to say they was the ones who collared the guy and done the county a favour by locking up another of these motor-vehicle felons. What they didn't say, at least not at that stage, was anythin' 'bout Lightnin' being black, but you guessed there was always a chance they were saving that one up for later.

They pushed their hats off their foreheads and said 'Okay boy, just step over here, we'll put a chain on them wheels to stop anyone stealing 'em whilst you-re gone, lest of course, they decide to set fire to it cos they can't steal it, but there ain't nothin' we can do about that.'

So Lightnin' stepped across and put his hands behind his back and had the cuffs slapped on his wrists as they pushed him down into the back seat of the po-lice car.

Which, Lightnin' figured, was the worst place to be doing any more talking, so as they swung the car round and went skidding off up the street, no-one said a word more about it.

Back in town they told Lightnin' to 'get out of the car and no funny business' walking him across the pen to the po-lice station where, flanked by three officers, they put him in front of a big desk with a big burly desk-sergeant stuck behind it and told the sergeant they'd rounded up another o' these motor-vehicle-felons and they'd best get him on a crime-sheet quick 'fore he come up with any more crazy ideas 'bout how to waste po-lice time.

The sergeant took one of those long rolls of paper with the carbon underneath it from a shelf beneath his desk, tore off a strip and started to write something in the spaces, turning to Lightnin' to get some details about his name and for him to give his story about what happened, taking it nice and slow. So Lightnin' told him about how he was driving along the lane minding his own business and doing his best to avoid all them big holes they put in the roads round those places, and then swerving so as not to hit a little black pig that jumped out in front of him and then gone diving into a ditch before the po-lice come to ask him what he was doing in the ditch.

The desk-sergeant wrote a load more stuff on the paper and then looked up as they took Lightnin' along the corridor and put him in the cell taking the laces from his boots so as he couldn't go hanging himself and checking his pockets just to make sure he wasn't carrying anything that might come under the heading of 'contraband'. Then they left him lying there in the dark with nothin' to do other than wonder whether his car would be still stuck in the ditch when he got back to where he left it. And then thinking it might get to be a while before he'd be getting' back to where he'd left it, and that it seemed doing the best you can ain't ever going to be no guarantee of being anywhere near doing enough.

It was next morning they got Lightnin' out o' bed nice and early with a cup of water and a corn-biscuit.

'Okay boy, you're going to come with us.'

It was a different three officers who took Lightnin' and stuck the cuffs back on him and led him up to where the daylight was suddenly brighter than anything he'd ever imagined and stung his eyes, leaving him blinking and looking up at the desk-sergeant who was a different sergeant from the one who'd written his story down on paper when he'd first arrived.

'Right, this way boy.' Off they went, the po-lice leading the way, stood either side of him onto the busy road where heads turned and immediately looked away at the sight of another black man being bundled into the back of a po-lice wagon.

Next minute they was off screaming down the street once again, coming to a halt before the biggest and greyest-looking building Lightnin' had ever seen and telling him to get out of the car and no funny business and have him stand a moment beneath the Star & Stripes flying from the awning above where, for a few moments he would have the opportunity to look out on God-fearing, law-abiding folk going about their lawful business, and maybe gain something from the experience, before being led to a big black door which they opened and pushed Lightnin' through.

In they all went, Lightnin' first and then the three officers, all traipsing their way down some steps to a cell where they told him to sit right where he was, there in the cell and to wait there till they got back, which was all he could've done given no-one'd thought to stick a door in the rear wall so's he could make his escape out back of the building.

It was two to three hours later that they was back, this time to take Lightnin' from the cell and lead him back up the steps through another big door and then along a corridor and through another door and up some more steps where he found himself in the biggest inside of any building he'd ever been in. They took him past po-lice and lawyers and a woman tapping away on a machine and they led him up more steps and had him stand in a kind of box where he could do little more than put his hand on the rail and look to the front.

And then came this big announcement and everyone was told to get to their feet. And it was the judge who'd arrived, who – on taking his place behind a big desk and given his spectacles a good wipe – made it clear to everyone they were gathered in the courtroom to see justice being done and that it was all their duty to devote their energies to that end and nothin' else.

And on issuing the advice, hammered on the desk and looked down, checking that Lightnin' had been listenin' and was looking and feeling sufficiently contrite at what he was hearing.

And Lightnin' was looking up at the judge, and for some time they just sat and stood there looking at each other.

Which was where the judge – thinking maybe it was time someone said something – leant forward and spoke, his eyes bearing down on Lightnin'.

'Boy – you ever been up before me?'

The words rang round the courtroom so loud and clear it seemed Lightnin' needed to come up with an answer pretty darned quick. He looked up at the judge.

'I dunno,' he said. 'What time d'you get up?'

And for what seemed like an eternity you could have heard a dime coin drop on the floor of the courtroom and there wasn't nothing else said till the judge decided it was about time someone said something more and he looked down again, this time near enough falling out of his chair he was leaning so far towards Lightnin'.

'Boy – we don't like your kind,' he said, giving Lightnin' the meanest look, which was the biggest sign yet that it was to do with him being black – and had Lightnin' figuring if it was going to get said some place it might just as well get said right here in a 'Court Of Justice.'

And then – when the place had settled down and the judge told the po-lice to tell the court their tale and then peered over the counter and asked Lightnin' if he'd anything to add to the testimony they'd just heard and Lightnin' explained how he'd only been doin' the best he could and din't mean anyone no harm, the judge just gave him his meanest look yet and told him where he was going he wouldn't be doing anyone no harm for some considerable length of time.

Then brought the hammer slamming down on the desk and told everyone to get up on their feet because he was about to leave but he'd be back pretty darned quick to see justice done. Which was exactly what he did.

So – some time later as they led Lightnin' away to begin paying his dues – the moral of the story is....If you're driving along a country lane one day minding your own business and a little fat pig runs right out in front of where you're heading – run him over!

[Based on a joke I heard told by the American Bluesman Lightnin' Hopkins between songs in one of his concerts.]

⤸

Row Three – Seats Four And Five

'Okay honey, this way. That's right. Now – we need to make our way down a few more steps. Our seats are just down here on the left.'

The man issuing the instructions – a middle-aged man with light receding hair dressed in pressed grey trousers, collar, tie and polished shoes took a moment to check with the numbers on the end of each row.

'Seats fourteen and fifteen. Three more rows down and in we go.' His wife – a thin anxious looking woman reflected in her choice of lilac skirt, outdoor coat gloves to match and hair tied in a neat bow with a magenta ribbon – followed, led step by step, behind him.

'That's it, just grab my hand and watch you don't lean too far over, the seats are pretty close together here. That's it…Row Three, Seats Four and Five. Here we are. Right, you take this seat and I'll sit here. Yes, don't worry honey. I'm right here next to you. Let me take your coat, we'll put it over this seat. There's lots of space. They won't be using all these seats.'

On taking their seats there was an overwhelming urge to be seen keeping themselves occupied, repeatedly brushing themselves down and in her husband's case, flicking idly through the booklet they'd been handed back at the kiosk near where they'd parked the car.

His wife leant closer, a firmer grip on his hand enabling her speak to a little more easily. Her voice when it emerged was frail, forcing him to lean towards her to avoid the awkwardness of her needing to repeat herself.

He patted the hand and directed his eye to the focus of her question.

'Yes I know honey. You need to know what's here. I know that.'

He shifted to get a clearer view, initially focusing his attention on the area their side of the screen, aware of a need to engage in conversation but equally aware of a need to keep it low-key...

'Well honey, the whole place ain't that big, 'bout as big as one of them small roadside churches. They got it split into two bits. There's the sitting-bit, that's where we are. Then they got the main-bit which they got decked out to look like a stage, all lit up with stage-lights. They've got a screen between the two bits – a big see-through screen. I guess that's so we can see what's happening. In the booklet they gave us it don't say much about it, just calls it 'the screen.' I guess the idea is in time you just forget it's there. There's more seats on the other side but they're all empty. Guess it might be for the other family...No I don't know what's happening there; they didn't say nothin' about that. Ain't nothin' happenin' there yet. I suppose they ain't allowed to give too much away about what other folks have got planned. We'll just have to wait and see. Yes, I'll let you know honey; course I'll let you know if anyone else arrives.'

He turned to the front, tapping the booklet repeatedly against his knee, again needing to lean to his left to catch what his wife was saying.

'Yeh, it's okay honey I was just coming to that. Well like I say, the main bit's beyond the screen. They got two windows. I guess that's to let a bit of light in so it don't get too gloomy. And it's all tiled and real clean-looking, bit like one of those operating rooms in the hospital. And then – right in the middle there's this big silver chair with white pads, like a dentist's chair, leaning back to make it look kind of relaxing, like the most natural thing in the world would be to lie on it and drop straight off to sleep. And they got straps going across it. Maybe that's to make sure you don't fall out...They actually got a name for it...'

He stopped and leafed through the pages of the booklet. 'They got it written right here at the bottom of the page.'

He read slowly, not entirely sure of his pronunciation but not wishing to be heard getting it wrong. '*The Terma-Seattle Gurney.*' Sounds good the way they put it like that. They got this box at the side with switches and stuff. Guess it must have cost a few dollars to get the whole place rigged out like this. Then on the left they got two curtains. I guess that's so they can close them after, stop people looking in. And they got a clock too. They got that on the wall right opposite the chair. I guess it's important to know exactly what the time is just to make sure they get it right. 'cause they got to be strict in terms if timing 'cause of all the records and stuff. Part from that there ain't much happenin' there at the moment. Yeh, don't worry honey, I'll let you know when something's going on, course I'll let you know. We ain't come all this way just to have me sit here without letting you know what's going on.'

He at once reached for the booklet and waved it before her.

'I got the booklet right here.' It seemed only right to make it known he was in possession of the facts despite knowing there's no way she'd be able to avail herself of its contents.

'They give you the booklet so you know what's happening,' he said, flipping absently through the pages. 'I'll read you the important bits. Tell you what – I'll read you some of the bits now. I might just as well do that now, while we're waitin'. Just wait till I find the right pages.'

He skimmed through a page of introductions, skirting over the details and then onto the next page which he held open between them, making a point of its contents being for both their benefits.

'Okay honey they got somethin' here 'bout 'Witnesses'; 'cause that's what we are – officially, that's what we're known as...'witnesses'. That's what we all got to sign afterwards. Then they got a bit 'bout how they used to do it and how in some places they use a machine, like in New-Jersey and Missouri.' He reached across, the open page extended as an aid to grasping what he was saying. 'Says what they do is...each person presses their bit of the machine at the same time so they feel like they're all in it together, like it ain't just one guy.' He turned the page. 'Says that Illinois uses the computer and Missouri and Delaware use the manual switch. And how nowadays it's sometimes done on tv, like up in Illinois. Guess the tv's a good way of doing it so's people can see what's happening more easily. Then, next page, they got something 'bout Federal Law-Suits and a 'Lower-Cast' and some stuff about 'Amendments To The Constitution.'

He skipped the page, leaning towards his wife thrusting what followed before her unseeing gaze.

'They got a bit here *Meet The People*. That's the people they got working behind the scenes. They get a lot of people working on it. They got stuff on three of them: The Major, The Warden, the Correspondent-In-Charge – says they've each done at least a-hundred-and-twenty and they're all here making sure it gets done right, and then they got a whole load of facts and figures about it. Then...'

He stopped – motioning with his arm and straightening the page to ensure the bit that followed got read correctly. 'They got a bit here on what they do beforehand. It's right here. The phone call! They're talking about the phone-call. You remember the phone-call. Well they're talking about it right here. How it came about two-o-clock. You remember that. You was out back when it rang.'

He searched the page, not wishing for either of them to miss out on its details.

'Says they're allowed a visitor. Don't say who but I guess it was one of the guys they got listed on the other page. Maybe later we can ask who that was. I think it might be nice to know who the guy was. Maybe he'd let us talk to him. I think it would be a nice thing to do – to talk to the guy about what he was talking about.'

He leant closer still making a point of holding the page between them to have her feel part of what's going on.

'Says about four-thirty they give them something to eat, says they can pick what they want. Guess it'd be fried chicken. Fried chicken and french-fries.' He turned at the sound of his wife's voice. 'Yeh – pancakes too, that's right. With maple syrup.' He turned the page.

'What's that honey? Not sure about that. It don't say nothin' 'bout that. I guess it's just long baggy trousers and a baggy top. That's what they give them to stop them getting too sweaty. They've got to keep them comfortable, you know so they ain't sittin' there scratching away when they're sitting talking to the guy.'

It was some time later that a disturbance behind prompted immediate investigation. Three figures – all mid to elderly – two males, one female, stepped into space at the top of the steps led by a uniformed figure, then slowly made their way down the steps, each stepping carefully, conscious at being seen in a place that under normal circumstances they'd never be seen anywhere near but directed by circumstances beyond their control; every inch of their progress followed from the other side of the aisle. The men wore jackets, one looser than the other with dark grey flannel trousers. They let the woman in first – likely the first man's wife – wearing a three-quarter length skirt, matching top and a wide hat with a light blue ribbon.

Everyone watched – waiting till the seating was finally sorted, the occupants settled into place – only then, opportunity for fleeting eye-contact to be made across the aisle.

'I think it's them honey, I think it's their people,' he said, able now to breathe a little more easily and ease the grip on his wife's hand.

'It's okay honey. That bit's done now.'

On both sides there was a feeling of intruding in someone's privacy, like peering into a burgled room waiting for something to happen – no-one wishing to be the one to break the spell by drawing unnecessary attention.

A shared sense of relief when some moments later there was a movement beyond the screen: a buzzing noise followed by a door clanking open and shut. A uniformed officer followed by a second officer was clearly visible stepping into a narrow hallway ahead of a third figure – barely visible from the seats – shuffling alongside them, head-bowed.

The grip tightened on his wife's hand.

'It's okay honey. I think it's him. It says they call his name and he gets to go with the guy.' Three figures were seen forming a line and then stepping forward at a signal from somewhere off-stage – making their entry, heading for the bed waiting in the centre.

'Yeh. It's Billy. Billy's coming now!'

Sighs and exclamations one side of the screen were met by movements beyond it, each adopting his appointed position, centre-left for the first officer.

'It's okay honey. I got it right here. Yeh, course you can. Go on, that's okay. No-one's looking. Don't matter anyway if anyone's looking. You ain't doin' any harm. Don't know if he can see you from his side. But you never know. You never can tell. Maybe he's looking right this way.'

There was further movement – a figure stepping into position to the right of the bed, voices exchanged, inaudible beyond the screen.

'Okay, he's got guys standing by him. Now they've moved round a bit to the right; guess they need to make a bit of space. Now they're stood still again...No, his hands are down by his side. Huh? Oh he's looking real calm honey – real calm.'

On what appeared to be a count of three an officer escorted Billy to his place, easing him to a sitting position for some adjustments to be made behind.

'Don't worry honey, I got it right here. What they do is get Billy into place, getting him to lay down on the bed with his head on the pillow. That's what they're doing right now. Yeh, he looks real peaceful. I can see the 'Right-Side' person now – that's what they call him – just stepping back a little and getting

Billy's head settled on the pillow. Guess they're telling him what to do…'lay your head this end son, and your feet that end'. Now they're doin' his wrists. Says here they got two belts – one across the left shoulder, another across the abdominal area, guess that's down here. Seems like they already done that bit; got Billy strapped down good and tight so he can't come to no harm…Huh? I don't know about that honey, you can't see everything from here. He just looks real peaceful okay? Looks fine. Looks like his head's moving around a little from side to side that's all. Now they got him to keep his head nice and still. That's it, you keep your head nice and still Billy. Now he's looking up, looking the guy right in the eye. I think he said something then…What? No I couldn't make out what he was sayin'. Maybe they'll tell us afterwards what he said. It'd be quite nice to know what he said to the guy. Maybe 'Thankyou sir' or something like that. It says here that's the kind of thing they say when they're strapped down tight. Okay – the guys have stood back now. Now they're all stood back and now there's other guys. Let me see what it says. I guess it's the medics, they got medics on-hand, all sides. What they gotta do is…establish IV contact. No, I'm not too sure 'bout that either. But that's what it says here in the booklet.

Yeh okay honey…I can just see what they're doing. Like it says. They're wiping his arm. Wiping it with what it says here – alcohol. Sterilization see honey. What it says is… 'cann-ul-ae are sterilized during manufacture'. I guess that's a good thing, making sure everything's clean. Now – something else is happening. I saw a guy say something. I think maybe they're slipping the first needle in honey, slipping it in real slow. No that's okay, you go ahead. Seems like that's the first shot – says here…Sodium Thio-pent-al – typical dose 3 – 5 mg/kg. I guess that's what they're giving Billy, 3 – 5 mg/kg. Now they got someone pressing down below his knee. I don't know what happened there, I can't see everything, I think maybe his leg got a bit twitchy. Now they got two more guys coming over. Says here a guy from KSAM, don't know who the other guy is.

Seems like they're keeping an eye on things, making sure they're doing it right.

Says they got two tubes – two tubes going into Billy's wrist. Yeh, I know honey. No, I don't know exactly where the tubes go either. Just says a line from the IV line is attached and secured to Billy's wrist. Seems there's a lot going on but that's the way they gotta do it. What it says is…they've got to check the connections, make sure things don't get mixed up. No I ain't sure 'bout what that means either. Tell you what though honey – seein' Billy lyin' there like that, I ain't ever seen him lying still as that, not even when he was a kid. You remember when he was little lying in his cot with that monkey-doll we got him from town. You know he's still got that thing. Maybe we should've brought the monkey-doll and put it beside where he's lyin'. Though maybe they don't let you bring things like monkey-dolls in. Seems strange seein' him lying there surrounded by folks who ain't gonna have much more to do with him. What's that honey? Yeh. I don't see why not. Don't say nothin' about it here. And we don't know whether he can see you or see anyone now but that don't matter; maybe he can, maybe he can't, ain't no way of knowing about that.

Huh? Yeh…three shots, one after the other. That's the way they do it.

Right now they're stepping round him again. Now the're back honey; one guy's right next to him there on the right. Now there's another guy. Yes – I can see it now. Guess they're givin' Billy his second shot – says here 'non de-pol-arizing muscle relaxant'. Guess that's what they're giving Billy right now. Says it helps him stop breathing, making him nice and drowsy. Seemed he was looking pretty drowsy before they give him the shot. No – he ain't doin' nothin' now – just lying there. Now they gone to one side looking at this screen, maybe it's a kind of x-ray thing showing Billy's insides and stuff.

Says here it relaxes the muscles – sustained something or other of the muscles. Yes – seems like Billy's muscles are done now honey, sustained...or whatever it is, seein' him lying there like that. But that don't matter, that's the way it's supposed to be. Now they gone back to the box to check on how things are doing.

Now they're back again. Now it's the guy giving the shots back to Billy. I can't see what he's doin'. Guess they're givin' Billy his third shot...Yes – I guess that's what they're doin' – givin' Billy his last shot. No I can't see exactly but they got it right here. `Potass'um chloride`. You heard of that? I've heard of that. That's what they just give Billy for his third shot. Says it stops Billy's heart from beatin' no more. That's what it says – right here in the booklet.

Yes – I am honey, I'm looking at him right now. He's lying there and looking real peaceful, real quiet. Yeh, I know honey, I know...It's okay...it's okay. I can't see that either.

What?...The guys are all back at the machine now. They're all stood round staring at the machine, seeing what it's sayin' 'bout Billy. No I don't know honey, I can't see too good from here. Maybe they'll tell us later what they're looking at. What it says right there on the screen. Maybe they got somethin' about it in the booklet.

Something else is happening now. The lights have dipped. Yeh – now they're closing the curtains. Huh? Yeh...course you can honey. Ain't nothing in the booklet about not doin' that. I don't know. Maybe he can, maybe he can't. Ain't no way of knowing about that. They've drawn the curtains now, just like it says in the booklet. Now all the lights have gone.

Come on honey, we can go now. Ain't nothin' to say we can't get up and go now it's all done. That's right. Don't forget your bag. We gotta go and see the guy remember. That's what they said we gotta do. We got to sign the book or the document. That's like everyone has to do. Huh? Yeh, I guess they gotta sign it too. I guess everyone's got to sign the book just to say it was done right. Yeh, I got your coat. That's it, grab my hand. Watch you don't lean over too far. That's it.

'Hi...' That's the other folks honey. They're leavin' too. 'Yeh...Yeh. That's what we were sayin. Yeh, it went good...real good.'

That's the other folks, they're leavin just ahead of us. They were sayin' it seemed to go good. I said yeh, that's what we was sayin'.

Okay we'll just get up the stairs here. You take it easy now. Okay.

It's okay honey. Their people have gone through the door now. We gonna go that way too so we can sign the book okay? Just take my arm. Tell you what honey – how about after we're done we go and find a diner in town? Order fried chicken and French-fries like they would've give Billy to eat. Yeh, that's right – pancakes and maple-syrup too, just like Billy would have done it. Huh? Yeh, it's looking real good, real bright and sunny out there. Yeh, I know, just how Billy would have liked it. Okay we'll just follow these guys. What? No don't worry about that honey. Ain't no way we're gonna get lost. I got the booklet right here, open on the right page, don't you worry about that.'

❧

The Happiest Man Alive

The man in a smart jacket and matching tie strutting through the door of the lobby of the hotel was arguably the happiest man alive. He was happy on two counts: *one* – his days of checking into soulless hotel rooms were numbered, *two* – the reason being, he was recently married, by some five weeks, and was already about as assured as a man can be that married life suited him just fine.

As the lobby door closed behind him and the all-too-familiar trappings of a life spent largely on the road were once again there to greet him: pseudo oak panelled walls, the pseudo-trendy bar with its line of innocuous lagers and last-ditch attempt at respectability in the form of a Guinness tap occupying its customary slot at the end of the line, he put his case to the ground to take a few deep breaths.

The man's air of exuberance wasn't solely on account of being married – it was as much the surprise at finding himself married. For truth be told, Norbert Carlisle had thought the chances of meeting a woman who would even prove a viable candidate as a long-term partner/wife were about as likely as him taking up residency on Mars! Let alone finding someone prepared to commit herself to such an arrangement. For being a simple man of a relatively simple disposition, he'd always seen himself falling some way short of most people's image of a 'woman's man' (however such a person could be accurately defined...strong, masterful yet sensitive to a woman's needs... perhaps.) Which wasn't to say he was any closer to most people's idea of a 'man's man' either; ie. always ready with a joke or some wry observation. Or some poignant observation on sporting matters, particularly football. He didn't actually know many women – or men – and knew virtually nothing about sport! Nor did he know many (if any) jokes. And as if to rub salt into the wounds, most of the people he did come into contact with – almost exclusively through work – were either married or had partners.

So it had been quite a red-letter day some three months previous when it transpired that not only did such a woman exist – a secretary to a law-firm who he had met on a delivery of a consignment of Christmas crackers and table-napkins for their annual 'hootenanny' in one of the town's up-market hotels – but following a brief courtship, had undertaken to do exactly that: step in to fill a void just when it seemed all prospects of such a thing happening were nil: A pleasant and remarkably astute woman, who'd listened attentively as he'd filled her in on a few details about himself, even remembering to pop in a question about how a good-looking woman like her came to be working behind a secretary's desk, which he thought was a pretty good line to be coming out with all things considered, and one that certainly seemed to raise a smile.

So, several weeks later, here he was – reporting for duty before hopefully the last in a line of anonymous-looking reception-desks to complete the formalities and on being allocated a first-floor room, opting for the stairs rather than taking the risk of riding potentially hazardous hotel lifts.

As the card slid into the slot and a green light and buzzing tone permitted entry, he pushed the door and took his first glance at the Spartan surroundings that would serve as 'home' for the next few days, dumping the contents of his travelling-bag on the few available shelves and seating himself on the bed to pass a few minutes with the hotel's 'Welcome' folder.

Which wasn't to say the days to follow would prove entirely fruitless. The morning's agenda of a more cost-effective approach to banquet-scale merchandising followed by a presentation of three-piece cutlery kits with a 'buy-and-take' feature aimed primarily at the overnight-stay end of the market – sounded promising and may well feature on next month's Long-Term Project-Management Working-Party's agenda.

With the morning's activities behind them it was during the afternoon presentation of Christmas napkins that he'd found himself next to an employee of one of their sister-companies. She too in marketing, but with an eye on potential foreign markets, mainly in the Far-East, where – interestingly enough – he'd pledged to undertake his own investigations once settled in his new post. A single woman with a cheerful disposition; having been allocated adjacent seats in the conference-room they'd hit-it-off pretty much on first greeting, swapping ideas on a range of subjects from kitchen-towel dispensers to potential targets in the Far East and Brazil as well as establishing contacts closer to home across The Channel.

It was in the midst of their exchanges over a cup of tea and biscuits that rumours began to spread, soon to be confirmed, that due to a union dispute in the firm providing the materials for the following day's programme, the materials couldn't be delivered as promised. And as a consequence the conference would, out of necessity, be curtailed after breakfast the following day as opposed to the day after – but with full assurance all appropriate claims would still be met in full.

It was unfortunate, for there had been a number of ideas to get through, but these things happen and no sooner had the announcement been made than Carlisle was consoling himself with the prospect of arriving home a day earlier than planned, and as luck would have it, on one of his wife's days off – already picturing the scene as he burst through the door unexpectedly brandishing a big bunch of yellow flowers.

It was with almost a spring in his step that he returned to his room after the afternoon session determined to make the most of what few hours remained – a resolve to mastering the art of setting the shower at the right temperature before grabbing a quick forty-winks, even attempting (and most-likely failing) to get some joy out of the radio on the table by his bed.

In keeping with the generally upbeat mood even the hotel restaurant's 'special offer' for evening meal: *Fisherman's Pie and fresh-picked Norfolk garden-peas* proved surprisingly palatable, and the woman he'd met earlier at the seminar, and agreed to meet for dinner, proved to be convivial company. They'd enjoyed a drink after the meal and promised to keep in touch once they'd gone their separate ways, though whether either of them would keep their promise remained to be seen, particularly in light of him being a married man.

All that remained was a hotel bed – the loneliest of lonely places on such nights as this, a notion that would barely have crossed his mind two or three months ago. Whoever it was who said 'you only appreciate what you've got when it's no longer there to be had' clearly had climbing into a hotel bed alone late at night in mind. He kicked a few times against the sheets in an attempt to come to terms with what amounted to oceans of wasted space, flinging a few unwanted pillows in the direction of the tv screen and only after much tossing and turning and with thoughts of a more convivial night to follow – finally lulled himself into a deep and dreamless sleep.

Not unusually when away from home he was up with the lark and having shaved, packed and got himself ready for departure, descended the stairs to take his seat in the breakfast room where he'd agreed to meet the lady from the previous day. English breakfast for two was followed by a brisk walk round the grounds and a quick browse of the hotel's shop in search of a suitable gift to take home for his wife, consensus being that a china tea-pot or the set of place-mats with a picture of the town's famous castle would prove ideal choices. But then why force yourself into making choices when you could save time and trouble by taking the pair – gift-wrapped into the bargain?

An hour later, back in the car with their goodbyes behind them and a Neil Sadaka CD slipped from its case and popped into the slot – a near-empty road promised to get him to the ring-road with ample opportunity to keep an eye out for a florist, or at least a place that sold flowers: a petrol station or one of those road-side kiosks, the kind of place you got on the busier long-distance stretches.

A check on the watch told him it'd be about a three-and-a-half to four hours drive, maybe stop for a coffee halfway. That sounded like a good idea – a brief stop, maybe grab a sandwich, something to keep him going till he got back.

As ever, hearing the car slip into top gear was the signal to sit back, relax and give a little more thought to his future plans.

First on the agenda was Christmas. Being only three weeks away he'd get the decorations out tomorrow; check the lights to make sure all were in working order. Christmas itself would be a mix of the familiar and the new: Christmas Eve at home wrapping each other's presents, hopefully in private – and over a glass of mulled wine he mused, quietly tapping the steering-wheel in time with the closing bars of *Standing On The Inside*. Christmas-Day itself would be split – turkey in the oven overnight, veg ready first thing. Then – an hour or two with his wife's parents before getting back for roast turkey and all the trimmings – just the two of them: a special moment being their first Christmas together; assuming she was in agreement, which she'd appeared to be when he'd first raised the suggestion. Marriage is, after all, a partnership which means a little give-and-take on both sides.

With thoughts of Christmas behind him for now, it was back to thoughts of his short and longer term projects at work…

'Short-term' projects invariably came under the 'lower budget' bracket, currently – a range of table-mats on the theme of Merry or Elizabethan England. The idea being to raise the profile of what are commonly perceived to be little more than cosmetic peripheries – table-mats, napkin securers – to a significant contributor to the overall ambience of the occasion.

Close on its heels was the issue of disposable beakers at automated dispensing-machines. His theory, and one he would pursue once established in his new post, was that a contract for a more durable plastic to replace the traditional (and hopelessly inadequate) cardboard cup *was* do-able, it just needed to be thoroughly researched and negotiated through all appropriate channels.

Longer-term projects included a re-evaluation of the whole disposable-cutlery market – hopefully a nail in the coffin for the plastic excuses for knives and forks that snapped under the slightest pressure yet were still the obvious – or maybe 'only' – choice for the majority of fast-snack outlets. Discussion with Miriam – the lady he'd met back in the hotel – had confirmed they'd been thinking along similar lines, awaiting results on a more durable material, possibly in line with the three-piece kits featured on yesterday's agenda.

Like all these things, it came down to finance. But equally – planning, expansive research and ultimately gauging your target-audience – something he'd been stressing for years.

He beat a few more bars and as often on these occasions, found himself returning to matters a good deal closer to home.

First and foremost – starting a family: interesting choice of word he'd always thought…'start' a family, as opposed to… 'finishing' one? Anyway, however one termed it, children would certainly be arriving on the scene before long. Two he'd thought would be about right: a boy followed by a girl, the boy about two or three years older. Or possibly – three: two boys, one girl. Or – two girls. But then, which to come first, boy or girl? A tricky conundrum that was a little difficult to legislate for; unlike the issue of names – which again had him tapping the wheel and revisiting one or two ideas from his last trip. Robert was a possibility though he still thought sounded a little dull; maybe Roderick, or Lionel. Or maybe his father's name – Selwyn. For a girl, Valerie. He'd always liked the way three syllable female names rolled so easily off the tongue. Or possibly Blanche or maybe Mabel, both names you rarely heard these days.

He allowed himself a chuckle. This time last year if you'd have told him he'd be driving along the motorway in twelve months time thinking of names to give his kids he'd have said you were barmy, which just goes to show how foolish it is to take any of these things for granted.

His thoughts were interrupted as the CD came to a stop. He hummed gently, beating a few closing bars of *Hotel California* into the steering wheel whilst searching the shelf for a worthy successor, finally reaching for *Band On The Run* to get him through the final stretch.

Then there was the house to consider. He'd landed on his feet there he'd have to admit. `Much gracias Mother`, he suddenly found himself coming out with for some obscure reason. Not that there wasn't work to be done: a few rooms needed decorating: the kids' nursery for a start. And the garden needed a bit of attention; a new out-house – or summer-house as his wife insisted on calling it – a possibility. Something she'd been badgering him about for a while now. One thing she wasn't short of was coming up with plans for the house. Her point being – even simple improvements can reap dividends and delays in getting them underway simply added to future costs.

It was about three-quarters through the second half of the CD that he turned into his road, running his eye along the neighbouring gardens before approaching his own driveway.

First surprise had been finding a silver BMW parked right where – ninety-nine times out of a hundred – he'd have been parking his own more modest Fiesta. Thinking it a little strange to see a vehicle parked outside his front door like that, he stepped from his car, grabbing the present and bunch of flowers and making a stealthy approach to the house in preparation for giving his wife the kind of welcome she'd hopefully remember for a while.

It was the aroma of coffee and strong cigarettes that met him as he pushed open the door to the kitchen.

Strange, he thought. Still – he was back and delighted to be so. And on stepping into the hallway and establishing his wife was nowhere to be seen in the living room or kitchen and still keen to keep as low a profile as was feasible, clutching the flowers tightly in his right hand, he made his way up the stairs holding his breath in readiness for what was to follow....

'Darling!'

Suffice to say…nothing in this world could have prepared him for the moment he flung open the bedroom door to be greeted by the sight of his wife naked and on all fours – being taken from behind by a man gripping her round the waist with thick ape-like arms.

No words, no explanations to avoid him dropping to his knees and plummeting head-first onto the recently-fitted shag-pile carpet.

A few feet beyond which there was a scene of consternation: a cessation of their activities – the pair collapsing on the bed and reaching for shirts and nightgowns conveniently discarded by the bedside table.

For some moments the pair lay speechless, the whole scenario exceeding anything they could have envisaged. It was the man who – maybe feeling some greater responsibility – was first to acknowledge that someone needed to say something.

'That the guy?'

She nodded, taking a Marlboro from the packet and lighting it with the aid of his huge fingers.

'Sells – what was it you said…kitchens___?'

'Tablecloths, napkins….that kind of stuff!'

'Jesus Christ,' he exclaimed, sitting up and planting a pair of huge feet on the carpet.

'Nice little place though, he said, looking round. 'Used to be his mother's huh?'

'Yeh,' she said hurriedly, flinging the duvet aside.

'Come on, we've got to get him moved.'

He scrambled to the door, stopping only to pick up a bunch of yellow flowers.

'For you honey,' he said, grinning.

'Jesus Christ,' she said, turning to the door and reaching for her slippers.

(Note: what follows is [at the time of writing, at least,] entirely fictional...though based on a few real-life observations of the time.)

It is the year 2008. In its unstinting drive to raise standards and in-line with its policy to facilitate greater pupil involvement in school policy/inspection procedures, the government has initiated a new and quite radical (not to say 'controversial') procedure whereby secondary schools would designate a named pupil to shadow a senior teacher – quite likely the headteacher – going about his daily duties: a route to bridging the divide between 'supplier'...and...'consumer'. A voluntary scheme. But – with the carrot of participants being awarded... 'Academy Evaluation Status'...formal recognition as an active participant in the project, to be included on web-sites and all formal communications; a key-contributor to maintaining a successful working relationship between the constituent elements of the organisation...

The Headmaster's Day

My name is Edward Creamer. Some of the kids think it's a funny name and sometimes laugh about it. I'm not too bothered. They can laugh at it if they want. I'm not often with them at the moment and I won't be for a while because I have a special job. I'm the Headteacher's Designated Pupil Envoy. I learnt the word and how to spell it because it was on the letter I had to take home to my mum. It's an idea that the government started. The letter said I would have a function. My mum didn't really understand it but she just ticked the box that said *I agree to my child being the Headteacher's Designated Pupil Envoy,* then finished making tea. Next day I had to take the letter back to school.

A few days later a bald man with glasses came to see me and sat me down and said he was going to explain my function, which maybe he did and maybe he didn't, I couldn't really tell. He said it was to do with the government fronting-up and I would be like Mr. Allinson's shadow, following him. And it is up to Mr. Allinson if there are times he doesn't want me following him; that it was all part of my function. I nodded. He said I didn't have to write everything down because that would be too much to do, but at the end I could write down my feelings about what I'd seen if I wanted to and there would be an interview. But it would be secret and wouldn't be for 'general consumption.' Then he looked at me and didn't say anything so I nodded. He said to think of it as my contribution to the next phase of the Great Debate – a cog in the wheel in the strive towards a more open society. And did I understand what he had been telling me? I said no I didn't understand what he had been telling me, but he said that's okay, it doesn't matter.

But I quite liked the idea of being Mr. Allinson's Designated Pupil Envoy because it gets me out of some lessons for a while. If I'd been a clever pupil like John Savage or Melanie Whipsnade I wouldn't have been asked because they have to pass exams and go to university. But I'm not likely to go to university and when The Headmaster – Mr. Allinson got me in his office and said...Edward my boy there's something happening that you might like to be part of and would I like to be a part of it? I said yes because I liked the idea of being part of something and it would get me out of some lessons so I said 'Yes I would like to do that' and The Headmaster said 'good boy' and then told me what I'd have to do.

He told me I'd have to look, listen and take things on-board. Then he chuckled to himself and said I was going to be allowed to listen to what him and some of the teachers were saying. But not always; like I wouldn't be allowed to go in the staffroom and listen to what the teachers were saying there: about what they'd been doing last night like going out and getting drunk or taking their wife out for a meal or to the cinema or like Mr. Sykes who sits up all night playing War-Games on his computer with a man in Bolton. Mrs. Magwich who is a nice teacher says in the morning the teachers all stand round the board to see if they have to do a lesson where there is no teacher, and Mr. Owen who's from Wales looks round all the teachers and says 'they got me again, they got me again, three times this week.' But no-one's listening because no-one cares if he's been got three times that week, only if they've been got. I'm not allowed to listen to that or to go in the staffroom at all.

When Mr. Allinson asked me I didn't understand why he'd picked me because though I'm not stupid I'm not very clever either, and maybe a cleverer person would be a better Designated Pupil Envoy. But Mr. Allinson shook his head and said it was nothing to do with being clever; that they needed someone who they thought could do the job and tell it like it is and be trusted not to tell lies and I said I wouldn't tell lies because telling lies is wrong. He patted me on the head and said 'there's a boy'.

The other thing he said was that a Designated Pupil Envoy might sometimes hear things that shouldn't go beyond the school walls. He looked at me and didn't say anything for a minute and I understood what he meant and nodded my head when he said it. He said that's *exactly* why I'd been selected, which I also didn't understand but maybe you didn't need to understand everything to be the School's Designated Pupil Envoy.

It was my first day as Mr. Allinson's Designated Pupil Envoy. I wore a clean shirt and tucked it in before I knocked on Mr. Allinson's door. He said 'hello young man' and told me to take a seat. He told me I'd be hearing things that school pupils didn't often hear and I wasn't to repeat what I heard except maybe when the bald man with glasses came back to speak to me, and I said 'Don't worry Mr. Allinson, I won't say a word to anyone.' Then I took a seat and took out my notebook and my pen just in case I had to write anything down. Though I'm not very clever I can hear things well and I've got a good memory.

He said 'there's a boy' and then there was a knock on the door and it was Mr. Callaghan who is one of the Deputy Heads though they don't call them that any more and most of the kids like him. He's big and sweats a lot in Summer and often breathes heavily because he works hard. He said hello to me and then said he had something to get us off on the right foot. He looked at me and then at Mr. Allinson and said something to him and Mr. Allinson nodded. Then he told Mr. Allinson how the previous day a boy in Year Ten had told his form teacher to f-off because he'd asked him to take his coat off. They both looked at me and said I mustn't mind hearing that sort of word because being a School's Designated Pupil Envoy meant I'd be hearing about things I'd never heard about in school before. I said I didn't mind because I'd heard the word before and it doesn't necessarily mean you're a bad person if you say the f word, only of you use the c word.

The boy had told his form-teacher to f-off and Mr. Callaghan said they had to do something because there was a lot of this kind of thing happening. He asked if they could sent the boy home for the day and Mr. Allinson said yes, but they had to be careful because the Governors had said there are too many children being sent home and Mr. Callaghan rolled his eyes and clicked his tongue and said maybe the governors or the politicians would like to come in and be told to f-off several times a day in place of the teachers. Anyway, the boy was going to get sent home to show the class that telling their form-teacher to f-off wasn't allowed.

When Mr. Callaghan had gone Mr. Allinson got out of his seat and went to stand by the window. He just stood there staring outside and didn't say anything for quite a long time.

When he looked back he was looking at me with a fed-up look like maybe he was feeling fed-up about the boy telling his form-teacher to f-off but didn't know if he should be telling me because it was nothing to do with me, even if I am a Designated Pupil Envoy. And when he asked a question it was almost as if he didn't expect me to answer it. He asked me if I could tell him what was wrong in being asked to take your coat off in registration and shook his head and I said there was nothing wrong and it sometimes gets hot in school and I wouldn't want to wear my coat when it's hot.

Mr. Allinson nodded and stood a bit longer at the window before he came back to his desk and showed me a picture of his wife and their daughter. He asked me where he should put the picture, left or right or in the middle of the desk. I said it didn't really matter. He said he'd put it in the middle – for now at least. He then held the picture up and said could I imagine the girl in the picture, his daughter, who was only eight and looked like a nice little girl, telling her teacher to f-off because she'd been asked to take her coat off in class. I said no, I couldn't imagine that because she didn't look like the sort of child who'd tell her teacher to f-off, but then I'm a boy and it's different when you're a boy.

Next Mr. Allinson had to open some of the letters on his desk and said he was allowed to tell me about some of them. He told me the first was about 'Inset'. I know what that is because it happens a lot and we have to take letters home about it. It's when there is no school for the pupils because the teachers are told how to be better teachers. Mr. Allinson read the title aloud 'Across The Curriculum In Language Competence...The Next Step.' He showed me the page and read it to me again. He said it would go to the Head Of English because anything with the word 'language' in it always went to her. Then he opened the next letter which was called 'Preparing Your Bid For Specialist Status.' He read the title and the letter and then sighed and then said it was typical of the times: giving yourself a fancy label that would make no real difference to anything except let headteachers like him do what the hell they wanted, like fool around with people's jobs so they don't know whether they're coming or going and the politicians like to give the headteachers powers that they shouldn't necessarily have and sometimes can't cope with, and all to get everyone thinking things are happening for the better when really they aren't. And did I agree. I said yes, I did agree. He chucked the letter in the bin. I asked him if I should pretend I hadn't seen him chuck it in the bin. He said No – definitely not.

Then he came and sat by me and gave me one of his looks where his eyes go narrow like he was going to say something important. He said 'Ted lad, we – me and you – are a team, and together we're going to show everyone out there…He nodded at the window…how it really is! I nodded. I think he meant there was no point in me being there if I didn't see things like stuff being chucked in the bin.

Then he showed me a picture on his wall – his cottage in the south of France. It looks a nice place in the middle of fields. He told me that in the Summer holidays him and his wife drive for hours down country lanes and stop at tiny villages where they drink a glass of red wine and eat bread and cheese from the café for lunch and then lie in the sun and then in the evening have a nice meal and another bottle of wine. He said it was all part of his long-term project. I didn't understand but I don't think it mattered. Then he said I was a good listener and I said 'yes' and he smiled and went back to the window to look at the new Science block which is costing a lot of money and isn't open yet. I got the feeling he liked looking out of the window because there was no-one looking back and asking him lots of questions.

Then he turned to me and asked if I had any idea about what schools used to be like. I said did he mean in the olden days. He laughed and said 'sort of'. He told me that a long time ago when he was a normal teacher things were simple. That when a kid was naughty one of the men teachers like a PE teacher would grab the boy and pin him to a wall and warn him that if he was naughty again he'd get thumped and thumped good! And that it usually worked. I can imagine it would work quite well. If I was pinned to a wall by a big teacher and told I was going to get thumped and thumped good if I was naughty I don't think I'd be naughty. But maybe it's different with me because I'm not really one of the naughty ones. Or maybe they'd laugh at my name instead!

He looked at me.

'Now...the kid'd scream 'Where's my targets?' 'Where's my targets?" Then he laughed again. And I knew what he meant because we get lots of *targets* and I get them on my reports and *objectives* in the lessons that the teachers write on a screen at the front of the class and are what we're supposed to learn in the lesson, even if the kids aren't listening and throwing stuff round the room.

He came and sat by me again and his eyes went narrow like earlier which meant he was going to say something else I needed to listen to. He said not to get him wrong. He knew we couldn't go around pinning naughty kids against the walls any more. But he was trying to make a point how things were different – like in lessons. How when he'd started teaching many years ago all you got to teach with was a set of worksheets, or half a set and they'd be dog-eared, which means old. Now it was all interactive white-boards with cartoon characters bouncing round screens like watching Popeye, and then he stopped and said did I know who Popeye was and I said no and he said it was a sailor who had big muscles from eating lots of spinach. When I get home I'm going to tell my mum to start buying spinach when she goes shopping instead of beans.

But I know about the white-boards. We have them in some lessons, usually with younger teachers who use them all the time. Some older teachers don't use them at all because they don't know how to use them or how to switch them on. Mr Williams – our English teacher last year – said he hates the bloody things. I think it's because he couldn't switch it on and didn't know how to use it. But instead of using a white-board when he reads stories he does all the voices, so most of us listened anyway.

By now it was time to leave Mr. Allinson's office. Year Assembly had started. But because I'm Mr. Allinson's Designated Pupil Envoy I don't go to Year Assembly.

We walked past the classrooms where it was mostly quiet. It's usually quiet first thing in the morning because the naughty kids are still half asleep. Instead of being naughty they just slide down their chairs at the back of the class and pull faces at each other.

When we got to the English Office Mr. Allinson stopped me and said 'Tell you what Ted, we'll have a bit of a laugh.' He was smiling. I thought maybe he was going to tell Ms. Davis the Head Of English, and my English teacher, a joke, but it wasn't that.

He knocked on the door and winked, then opened the door and went in. Ms. Davis is a loud woman who isn't very old. She has short hair and starts her lessons by reminding us she's in the business of giving us the tools and that it's up to us to put them to good use. She says education is about empowering people to protect their interests. I know this because I had to write it on the first page of my English book and learn it for homework.

Mr. Allinson winked again and told Ms. Davis what I was doing there with him, that I was the Designated Pupil Envoy. She was putting stuff in her locker and stopped and shook my hand and said I was in a position to make things happen and I should value that and thank God someone somewhere was finally listening.

Mr. Allinson gave her the Inset letter and winked at me again. She waved the letter in the air and looked at him and then at me. I thought maybe she thought I'd posted the letter. She took a lot of stapled papers from her locker and shook them at Mr. Allinson saying she was fed up with being presented with rubbish and the people who wrote the rubbish were more stupid than the stuff they were writing. Then she shook the papers again and said it was from someone called 'The Campaign For Real Education' who said children must learn how to do grammar before they can write and what did Mr. Allinson think about that. Then she waved the papers at me and asked me what I thought because, at the end of the day, I was the one being screwed. She was looking at me and said 'Teddy-Boy (which is what she sometimes calls me) 'you're going to hear some *real* English now...!' Then she said 'Okay – here's a sentence...It is a dog....or...It is a fucking big fat ugly bastard of dog! Where exactly does technical nous step in? Tell me that Teddy my boy.' I shook my head because I didn't know and then she calmed down a bit. I know Ms. Davis gets angry about some things. Like when Michael Keighley drew a woman's chest and private parts on his English book she called him a sexist dickhead and then looked at the picture and said if it was his girlfriend – or his mother, she needed urgent medical attention. Then she put him on detention for a week and promised to phone his mother.

Anyway, Mr. Allinson didn't have the answer either and when he suggested she might like to take charge of the Teachers' Training Day she said she'd rather not, though she didn't put it quite like that. Then Mr. Allinson winked and we left.

Back in the corridor Mr. Allinson looked at me and said 'she's quite a card Ms. Davis isn't she?' I nodded. Then he said we were going to inspect the New Science block.

On the way we passed two boys put out of their lessons for being naughty. Mr. Allinson told them they were wasting the only chance they got and they'd never get the time they were losing back. Then we moved on.

The new Science and Technology block is being built but it is taking a long time and usually there's no-one there. So I didn't know what there was to inspect but Mr. Allinson just pushed the doors open and we went along the brand new corridors where everything was white and smelt of paint. And there were tins and tools everywhere and long pieces of plastic. And in some places there were wires sticking out waiting to go inside machines.

We went in a Science room with long benches and stools and it was really bright in there and we sat on seats surrounded by sheets of polythene. It all smelt like the pottery-room we sometimes go to in Art. Mr. Allinson kept looking round and nodding and then he said 'What do you think Ted?' I said it was looking good but it would be better when it was finished. For one thing it was a bit cold. But that is normal in rooms in school. A lot of them are cold – or hot in Summer. I don't know if anyone – maybe the teachers or maybe someone else like the caretaker – knows that if it's too hot or too cold you can't concentrate and do your work. And maybe if they spent as much money on heating as on lots of fancy stuff we'd concentrate more and learn more. In Summer when it gets too hot we sometimes ask if we can take our ties off because we'd be able to concentrate more and do our work better, but the teachers say 'No, it's the school uniform' and 'Put that tie back on' if someone takes their tie off. And some boys (and girls) won't put their tie back on and get sent out of class and get told they're wasting a valuable opportunity. In RE when Mr. Swan said it, Aaron Wallcott turned to him and said 'So are you.'

I think Mr. Allinson liked going to the new block because it's quiet there and there was no-one knocking on his door and asking him things. I think he just likes a bit of peace and quiet which is what a lot of the teachers like because in their job they don't often get that. Sometimes they'll come in the classroom and say 'Now what we all need today is a little bit of peace and quiet – and that includes you.' Though I think it's mainly them that need it quiet rather than the kids. Mr. Allinson was staring at the clean tops and all the equipment still wrapped in packets and looking round the room's white walls and saying 'A whole new beginning Ted. That's what we're looking at here; a whole new beginning!'

And then it went quiet, and it was very quiet just the two of us sitting in the Science block and it felt strange because it was so quiet and empty like all the kids were waiting to be allowed in shouting and drawing stuff on the desks and sticking chewing-gum in the Bunsen-burner holes.

For some time Mr. Allinson just sat staring at the walls and saying nothing. Then he suddenly got up and said 'Come on Ted lad – back to reality!' so I got up and brushed some white dust off my trousers.

It was strange going through the doors back into the main school, like we were going back into the past, which in a way we were.

It was fairly quiet in the corridor where there were notices and posters on some of the walls. One said...

> *Are we having fun?*
> *Yes – We are having fun....*
> *Why are we having fun?*
> *Because Learning is...*
> *FUN!*

Though one corner had come away from the wall where the plasticine had gone dry.

Then I had to go to PE which I don't like because I can't run very well and look funny when I try and wondered if Mr. Walker, who is our PE teacher, might pin me to the wall and tell me I'd get thumped and thumped good if I didn't run better.

When I went back to Mr. Allinson's office he was sorting out some stuff and he rolled his eyes and said I might as well go to playtime instead of watching him sorting out his stuff, which sounded like a good idea. At playtime I can go with the other kids but I'm not allowed to talk about being a Designated Pupil Envoy because it's against the rules. I wouldn't want to break the rules but I don't think anyone would want me to tell them about it anyway. I met my friend Jimmy Hibbert and we went to the canteen where they have toasted sandwiches and some of the girls go on Facebook and tell each other about it.

I had to go straight back to Mr. Allinson's office after playtime. When I knocked he said 'Come in laddo' and I went in. Mr. Callaghan was with him and was breathing a bit more heavily than usual – and sweating. Mr. Allinson said something to him and he nodded and I was told to take a seat.

They were talking about some of the things that had happened in some of the classrooms where some children had been naughty. Mr. Callaghan had been supposed to teach Sixth Form but he'd had to leave them. He said a supply-teacher had walked out of a lesson because they were shouting things out and calling him names and then someone had flicked something at a light bulb and smashed it and no-one would own up and in another class children were chasing each other round the room and refusing to stop and there'd been bad behaviour in other lessons too and some of the staff had got together and Ms. Davis had said she wanted to see Mr. Allinson.

Mr. Callaghan stopped but he was still breathing quite heavily and for a moment neither of them said anything. Then Mr. Callaghan looked up and said he didn't want to be melo-dramatic or something like that. And said that he thought they were in danger of losing it; that the problems were getting bigger and were happening more often and a lot of the teachers were fed up and then he said he had a suggestion. I think Mr. Allinson was quite pleased that Mr. Callaghan had a suggestion because he didn't have one.

Mr. Callaghan said they could have a meeting with some of the teachers to see if they could come up with any suggestions about what to do about the naughty children and Mr. Allinson turned in his seat and brushed his chin and said 'yes...okay.' But he said they had to be careful because nothing gets teachers more excited than talking about naughty kids apart from changing the dates of the holidays and they didn't want everyone just telling everyone else about the bad things that had happened. So they made a list of teachers and Mr. Allinson said lunchtime would be longer.

I then had to go to my lesson because I still have to go to some of my lessons whilst I'm a Designated Pupil Envoy. I went to English where Ms. Davis reminded us – as she always does – that it was another day not to waste: to take the opportunity to grab the tools and do something fantastic with them. Darren Walker said something rude about Miss grabbing his tool but she didn't hear him. We had to get into groups and discuss what to do about the authorities threatening to chop down trees to make a motorway. Then she read us a poem about a boy's little brother who gets killed in a road accident. Then we went to lunch.

The teachers had been asked if I should be allowed to go to the meeting after lunch and most of them had said yes because otherwise what was the point in having a Designated Pupil Envoy and Mr. Allinson agreed because if they were going to play the game it meant seeing things as they really are – warts and all! And Ms. Davis insisted I was there because who had the right to decide what a Designated Envoy should or shouldn't be hearing? Not them – not anyone.

So I was allowed in but I was told by Mr. Allinson it was an important meeting and I mustn't tell anyone – even the bald man with the glasses – everything that was said; *especially* the bald man with glasses, said Mr. Callaghan. I don't think he likes bald men who wear glasses. Anyway the teachers said they wouldn't be saying anyone's name because it would be wrong to do that so I wouldn't know who they were talking about. I said I wouldn't tell a soul anyway and Mr. Allinson said 'good boy' and told me to take a seat.

I sat in the corner and listened. The teachers talked about why a lot of kids were naughty and then they talked about the teachers but they didn't say the teachers' names and said some are weak and some are strong and some didn't know the difference which was part of the problem. Ms. Davis said it was dangerous to talk in terms of weak and strong because of its connotations. I was listening but it really didn't matter what they were saying because a lot of what they were saying I didn't really understand – only bits. Some of the teachers said they were frustrated from being told lessons always had to be fun. But how can it always be fun without you going nuts? And Mr. Meakes who's a senior teacher said someone who spouts all this stuff should realise that learning is also about opening a book, reading it and doing notes about it or writing about it. And the teachers nodded.

Then Mr. Allinson turned to me and said that as a Designated Pupil Envoy maybe I had a contribution to make. And he asked me what I thought was a good lesson. I didn't know I was going to be asked any questions about lessons and I had to think for a minute and all the teachers were looking at me which made me nervous and go red and Mr. Allinson said not to worry and to take my time answering the question and not to answer it if I didn't want to But I thought it would be better if I said something because otherwise why was I there? So I said it was better if you thought the teacher was interested in you and liked you, or at least liked you a bit and wanted you to get good marks. And it's good if they try to make the lesson interesting but you can't always do that and some kids will wreck the lesson anyway because that's what they prefer to do instead of doing work, and especially if they can't do the work and know they won't get many marks. And I was told 'well done' and Ms. Davis pointed an arm at me and said are the politicians hearing this? And Mr. Allinson said 'Well done Ted…Good boy.'

Then they talked about other things they could do like rewards and detentions and some of the teachers patrolling the corridors and going into some lessons.

After lunch I went to my next lesson. It was quiet in the lesson, and in the other lessons – like someone had told the kids that things had gone too far and the teachers were in danger of losing it, and there'd been a meeting about them. There were teachers in the corridors and some went into the lessons where the naughtiest children were to be found. In Music I tried to imagine Mr. Hardwick – who is a kind man who is small and thin and lets us go into the hall and bang on xylophones – pinning Michael Sanderson – who's big and a bit of a bully and calls out all the time – to the wall and telling him if he was naughty again he'd get thumped and thumped good. I don't he would listen – or he would listen but he wouldn't stop being naughty and might do the same thing back to Mr. Hardwick

It was the last lesson and I had to go back to Mr. Allinson's office for the end of my first day as a Designated Pupil Envoy. He said 'Come in Ted lad.' And I took the same seat as before. Then he said he was going to take another look at the Science block and did I want to come with him. I wasn't sure but I thought it might be better to say yes, and something in his voice said he would prefer it if I went with him.

As soon as we reached the doors the brightness hit us – more than before because the sun gets brighter in this part of school in the afternoon. Everything was still and silent like a ghost town. When we got to the farthest point we stopped and stepped round some boxes and a chair that goes round and round. Wires stuck out from the walls and there were boxes of glass tubes on a bench. Mr. Allinson looked in the boxes and laughed.

'Impressive isn't it?' he said. I said 'yes.'

Then he smacked the box shut and looked to the window.

'A new beginning Ted. A brand new beginning.'

This time we didn't stay long. He turned and we left the new block and went back to his office. When we got there he asked me how I'd found my first day as a Designated Pupil Envoy. I said it had been interesting and he said it had certainly been that.

Then he went to look out at the car park and turned back to his desk. He took a pen from his drawer, which he told me had been a leaving present from his last school, and opened a writing pad and told me to watch closely.

Then he said 'I think our work's done Teddy my boy, don't you?' And I said yes, because it was nearly home-time and our work for the day was nearly done. He didn't say anything else for a moment, until, taking the pen and drawing the pad towards him he started to write, telling me he was writing to the Chairman Of The Governors and to the Chairman of the local authority telling them his day was definitely done.

Then he looked at me and at the picture on the wall.

He said 'I think the south of France is getting a bit closer Ted,' and carried on writing. And though he didn't say any more I think I knew what he meant.

Two Mini Biographies

It had been a long day. A bitter wind stirring itself across the northern continent, had, for some time, been bracing itself for a final assault on the south eastern corridor of England where – in the rapidly fading light of the estuary – two boys, hands held like two 'babes in the wood' tip-toed their way towards the first of its ripples of water lapping around clods of earth and pebbles reaching as far as the tiny stone wall. Whilst some way ahead of them – a cluster of distant lights dotted the horizon like a necklace of floating stars...

It was two-o-clock when we left school by the side door near the Music room. I know it was two-o-clock because I checked with my watch. We had to wait a minute then we walked up the street so that no-one, not any of the teachers would see us. If the teachers had seen us they'd have said... 'Hey you two, where do you think you're off to?' And we wouldn't have been able to say we're off to live in a caravan because they would have told us off and made us go back. But that's where we were going. To a big blue caravan near the beach where you can play and climb trees. But we needed to move quickly or we'd have been spotted and then we wouldn't have been allowed to go there.

We had to walk about three miles before we could stop which is a long way but we needed to get away from school as quickly as possible. We got to a busy road where there were lots of lorries and we sat at the side of the road and Terry took out a Kit-Kat and said it was the last we'd get to eat for a while until we got to the caravan, so we needed to eat it slowly. I didn't like this part of the road because it was busy, the lorries go past quick and don't know if anyone else is there and don't care if anyone's there. But I knew we had to go along the road to get to the sea which we would swim across to get to the caravan.

Terry, who is in the year above me at school, was watching the lorries and chewing on his bar of Kit-Kat. He was telling me about the caravan, how there were sleeping-bags and pillows – three pillows. I said I only want one pillow. He said I could have one pillow and if there was a pillow spare it would go on the seat to lean against when we were watching tele…

Then we needed to get going so he screwed the silver paper into a ball and threw it onto the road and I did the same and he said 'We need to get going because it might get dark soon.' I got up but my legs were aching and sore from all the walking. But I knew he was right; we needed to get going or we might not get to the caravan before it was dark.

We set off again, walking past the factory where they make the cars and cafes and small shops that have gone grey because of all the soot and smoke from the lorries. Walking along the road with the lorries going past made me more tired even though Terry was talking to me, telling me about the cooking ring you put the pan on to heat stuff up and there was beans and peas in the cupboard. And sausages. I like sausages. He said there were sausages in the tin with some beans and some with bacon in too.

It had been Terry's idea to go to his caravan one playtime when we were hiding behind the wall by the skip to shelter from the wind and the shouts of the other kids who sometimes come after us at playtime and shout things.

He said it was his dad's caravan – or at least he thought it was his dad's. A big blue and white caravan parked on the edge of an island where there were beaches and sea-walls to run along and jump over. His dad had shown him a photo of it on a visit to his flat. Said how he used to go there with his girlfriend. How it was near the beach with woods behind and in front of it was the promenade that stretched out into the middle of the sea. His dad had told him about the small boat with an engine that him and his girlfriend, Pat had sat in as the man had taken them across the water to get to the caravan.

I was listening to what he was saying but it was difficult to get a picture of it because I've never been to the seaside. I've only seen pictures of it, but hiding from the wind and the shouts of kids at playtime it sounded like a good place to go to. The only thing was his dad had gone, and taken the photograph with him and he hadn't seen him since.

I was trying to step in Terry's footsteps because it means you might have good luck and maybe things will go all right when we get to the caravan. Terry was saying they had bread at the shop which isn't far from the caravan and we can buy stuff there. I said I didn't have any money and he said there was money in the caravan, not a lot of it but enough – and we can use that to buy bread and beans and tins of soup. Tomato soup. I like tomato soup. He said there was a tele and at night we could watch Star-Trek and eat biscuits sitting on the seat with a pillow to lean on. And during the day there's a big wood behind the caravan where we could sneak up on people and they wouldn't see us. And the trees have got low branches so they'd be good for climbing. We could build a den at the top. It sounded good because we could do what we wanted. There'd be no-one to stop us and say we weren't allowed to do that.

I was getting tired from all the walking. After about three hours we had left most of the houses and now there were fields and fences by the road and the lorries weren't as noisy as earlier. We decided to hitch a lift but Terry said we mustn't tell the driver we were going to the caravan or we might get in to trouble but it was a lorry-driver who didn't say much. He just took us along the road and dropped us by a roundabout and then drove off.

When we went down another road a bus came and we got on the bus. I didn't know whether it was the right bus but it was going the right way and after a long ride we got off the bus and Terry stopped and said we were nearly there and we'd soon be at the sea.

It was starting to get dark and I was hoping it wouldn't be much further because I was getting tired and I didn't know it was as far as this and I was a bit scared being in a place where there were lots of fields and it was empty and dark and really quiet with hardly any people around. Only millions of stars, more than at home and Terry said they were millions of miles away and I believed him.

We had to walk a bit further then Terry stopped and we had to turn left down a path and we got to another small road and then found another path and then I saw the sea for the first time. I didn't know it was so big – or as cold as it was standing there on the path looking at it. Terry was looking out across the sea too and I think he was looking at the island and I think he wanted to get to the island as quick as he could because it'd be good there and we'd be able to get warm and please ourselves about what we did.

Then he pulled on my arm and said 'Come on we need to get going. It ain't too bad in the water, it's only cold till you get used to it. When you're used to it it ain't cold any more.'

I took a few steps further and we went on a kind of beach where there were millions of little stones that crunched when you walked on them. I was freezing but maybe when we got going to the island it wouldn't be as cold because we'll be swimming and that would make us warmer. I'm okay at swimming; I could swim for twenty lengths in the baths when we used to go there on Thursday afternoons and I got a sticker for it and a certificate to put on my wall.

We got to the water and we stood looking out across it. It was nearly dark by now and you couldn't see a lot – just one or two lights and a small cluster of orangey shapes which Terry said was the island. But all I could see was water – tons of it, all moving up and down and stretching as far as other countries.

Terry took my hand and said we needed to get going and drew me closer to the edge of the water. He was pointing across the sea to the small bunch of lights, telling me that was where the caravan was, by the lights on the edge of the island just next to the promenade. I was looking but I couldn't see it very well and then I was looking down and scuffing a few pebbles with my foot. I wished I'd brought my other sweater or maybe my parka; it was a new parka. My mum gave me the money to buy it a few months ago when she'd come home briefly. It was the last time I'd seen her.

'It ain't far,' Terry was saying. He was pulling me along and staring at the lights. He told me there was a heater in the caravan; his dad had told him about it. An oil thing with a big can under it. I was wiping my mouth because I was getting sore lips from it being so cold. I didn't know the sea was as big as it was and I could see the lights but they were still a long way off. Terry said they weren't that far and there was a kettle in the caravan and when we got there the first thing we'd do is make a cup of tea and have biscuits. I asked if they were chocolate biscuits because I like chocolate biscuits best and he said yes but I'm not sure he knew about that; I think he was just saying that.

He grabbed my hand again and pulled me towards the water which had started swishing round my shoes. I was taking little steps because that seemed the best way to move with the water all round us and it was suddenly colder and I was shivering more. Then he said we'd better take our shoes and socks off and put them behind a tub thing on the rocks. So that's what we did but it felt funny walking back on the stones and my feet got sore.

'Come on.' He was pulling my arm. We needed to get going quickly so we would get to the caravan quicker. He said there'd be dry clothes when we got there and we could have a cup of tea and watch tele.

By now I was shaking a bit because I was so cold and then we went deeper in the water where it was difficult to see more than a few feet because it was dark. We were holding onto each others' arms and I was looking out across the water. All I could see was a few lights which might have been the island, I don't know, I wasn't really thinking about that now.

The water was up to my knees and Terry was pulling my arm. He was saying that tomorrow we would catch some fish from the sea and have fish and chips for tea and I like fish and chips when you get it from the chip shop.

He told me to keep moving and to keep wiggling my toes. So I did that but it wasn't easy because of all the water. I didn't know the sea was that big, or that cold. On tele I'd seen people on their holidays swimming in the sea and it was hot and white and everyone was splashing in it and it didn't look anything like this. I think maybe it was a different sea to this one. All I could see was waves bobbing up and down and they were near to the top of my trousers. Then Terry stopped and said we'd better take our shirts off to make us swim better, but I wasn't sure about that because it was cold enough with my shirt on and taking it off would make it even colder. But he said it would be alright and once we'd got moving we wouldn't feel the cold any more which I was glad about because it was very cold standing there taking off my shirt. So we had to go back and stuff our shirts behind the tub thing on the rocks.

When we were back in the water he said we'd better empty our pockets, but I didn't have much in my pockets. He had some tissues and chewing gum wrappers and a plastic soldier. I had a few bits of fluff, some bits of crisps and a crumpled worksheet from school, the ones where you have to put words in the gaps. We opened our fingers and watched the bits spill onto the water where they bibbed and bobbed and then disappeared from sight.

Terry said there were games we could play in the caravan like Snakes & Ladders and Mousetrap which would be good if it was raining outside and we had to stay in the caravan. Then we went further into the water where we had been before but it was better this time because I was kind of used to it a bit so I went further and so did Terry until the water had gone over my trousers and it was like something really cold tickling me and I held my arms out to stop myself from falling over. And then it seemed like for a moment I couldn't breathe, but when I went in more it wasn't so bad even though it was dark and I couldn't see much.

Terry was telling me that when we'd finished catching fish we could climb trees because there's lots of trees by the caravan and we could make a den in one which would be somewhere to go in the day and then we'd have two places to go – the den and the caravan.

I told him I was sinking in the water and freezing cold. He said that was okay that's what happens just before you get going and I wouldn't be cold for long because once you get going you don't feel cold any more.

He was looking across the sea and saying the caravan was next to the promenade by the bunch of orange lights.

But I wasn't looking at the lights now; I was looking at the water which was up to my neck and Terry stopped and said we needed to start swimming and I nodded though I felt scared because my feet were still on the ground and when we started swimming they'd be off the ground and there would only be water and nothing else.

But he said he'd go first and I should follow and copy him and if one of us got tired we'd stop and have a rest because we could do that. The island wasn't that far and once we got going it would be okay and we wouldn't feel cold any more and when we got there we'd put clean clothes on and have a cup of tea and a biscuit – a chocolate biscuit to warm us up.

Then he said 'watch me' and he sank into the water and started reaching his arms into it and I did the same and at first it was freezing and the freezing water was over my shoulders and then I tried moving my arms but then suddenly the water was all over my head....

I don't know what happened next, but there was water everywhere and I tried to swim like I knew how to swim from the swimming-baths but it didn't work the same and I was under the water and I heard a voice and I think it might have been Terry's voice but soon I couldn't see him or really hear him any more...

And for some moments nothing much *did* happen. Just a tumbling, falling spluttering, until – a few minutes later and entirely at the whim of the ocean settling back into place around them – the two boys reappeared as two dark shapes bobbing gently on its surface.

They had reached a distance of twenty to thirty yards from the edge of the water. A few miles beyond which, the lights of the island had – at this hour – all but disappeared from sight.

᷍

(In the late 70's two young teenage boys attempted to swim across the Thames estuary to get to one of their father's caravan. They both perished in the attempt.)

Doing The Right Thing

At the side of a town's main street a figure stood by an ass tied to a post at the end of a porch. Attached to the ass was a cart laden with a bundle shrouded in sheets and held firm by corners knotted and weighed down by small stones.

The figure was male, maybe mid to late twenties, dressed in black and currently issuing instructions for the ass to remain where it was while casting a second eye over the cart to which it was tethered. The ass nodded, plonking a foot either side of its post as its owner nudged the hat a few inches up its forehead to read the sign above the door. The sign read

H Everson. E. French. Burial And Funeral Directors.
Established 1893

Which – he rightfully assumed – had to be the place; the place indicated by the men smoking cigarettes on the balcony at the far end of town when he'd asked directions whilst putting them in the picture regarding developments back home on his side of The Desert.

A few feet beneath the sign stood a large green door. With a further brushing of the hat and a finger drawn across the ass's floppy ear – the words of his recently departed father suddenly as resonant as a crescendo of drums – he made his way to the door, turned the handle and with a final glance back at the ass, disappeared from view.

In contrast with the street, a grimy indoor light dominated the scene broken by a line of cabinets stood aside a long wooden desk.

Two men were behind the desk. One standing – a large man with chest-height breeches and a tie, the other – a thinner, younger man with narrow eyes and smoking a fat Havana cigar. Both shifted forwards at the disturbance, the cigar chuffing thick wads of smoke in their visitor's direction.

On invitation to take a seat, he took his hat from his head and placed himself on a jittery wooden chair.

The men were saying nothing, sticking to a time-and-trusted principle of granting new-arrivals the privilege of opening proceedings – in the case of young to middle-aged males. With an elderly male it would be different, as with a female, particularly an elderly female, in which case they would find themselves doing near enough all the talking.

Eventually the man flipped a head over his shoulder toward the cart and its contents sitting in the street.

'It's my pa,' he said.

A long plume of smoke was followed by a long hard look in their man's direction and then to the street beyond the building's window.

'Your pa dead?'

There was a moment's hesitation before confirming the fact.

'Guess so.'

'That your pa lying on the cart?' A nod followed – a hint of embarrassment at having descended upon them in such ignominious fashion.

'When he die?'

'Some time last night I guess.' He stopped to recall the moment. 'I took him his morning tea but 'stead of reaching up to take it he just laid there staring at the ceiling. When I put the cup down and looked closer his eyes was all glassy and open.'

Another cloud of smoke erupted from across the table.

'What he die of?'

There was a hunching of shoulders.

'Dunno, weak heart maybe. Or maybe his brain went,' he said, these being the only organs of any significance to immediately spring to mind.

'Or maybe just too old.' There was a consensual nodding – from everyone, including the man stood hovering over the main man's shoulder.

'You want him buried huh?' There was relief at the prospect of turning their attention to more immediate matters.

'Guess so.'

The man rotated the cigar through middle and index fingers and turned to his partner, nodding for him to take something from one of the cabinets before raising himself from his seat to extend a hand across the table.

'Name's Everson,' he announced.

'Hope,' said the visitor, responding by rising from his seat to shake the hand. 'Jake Hope.'

'This is my partner Al Fish.' Fish reached across and shook the hand. Both men returned to their places. Everson tapped cigar ash in the dish and turned a few papers handed to him by his partner.

'Okay, you want your pa buried and you want him buried good.'

It sounded right enough. Such arrangements were likely routine to these guys and seemed unlikely to make too many demands on anyone's time.

'Okay.' Papers rustled in front of Hope's eye, both men preoccupied with finding whatever it was they were searching for amongst its contents.

'So – any thoughts about where you want your pa buried?'

There was a shifting in the seat opposite. This – above all else – he guessed he needed to be clear about, even though this too seemed a relatively straightforward question.

'With my ma.'

Hope had seemed to hesitate – aware of the need to be clear about these things yet not entirely confident of his ability to be so. The men's eyes rose.

'Where's that son?' The questions coming thick and fast were at least a sign they were getting somewhere, that it might not be too long before they'd be getting his pa on his way and the cart and ass back on their way home across the desert, hopefully before sundown.

'Cross the ocean,' he said, fiddling repeatedly with his hat. 'Home Of Our People – And Our People's People,' he added, passing an eye over the array of filing cabinets and legal documents as he spoke...Lines he could repeat with barely the blink of an eye given the number of times he'd sat back and heard his pa and the rest of their people regaling each other and anyone who happened to be passing of a commitment to...as it was commonly put 'do the right thing': a commitment to honouring Their People's eventual return to the one and *only* spot on the planet where – as was set in tablets of stone dated a few thousand years and more: death – the one true route to salvation – would find release to be at-one with their Maker, and in so doing, secure the path to true enlightenment and ultimate sanctity...or at least something along those lines!

All of which, at first glance, seemed like a straightforward enough proposition. Even if it *did* seem a little strange how some people – particularly older people – always appeared to get a good deal more excited about what lay in store for them when they were dead and gone than while they were alive and kicking. As far as he was concerned it was no great secret where anyone was heading when his time was done.

There was the tapping of a pen on the desk and a few whispers passed. Both men looked across but again it was Everson who seemed to assume the upper hand, leaning back to view Hope from a slightly different perspective; rule of thumb – always to take these things one step at a time, or as his father would have put it – 'never let the other guy know exactly what you're thinking.'

'Hmm...' he said, still thumbing his way through a few pages of print and then stopping to look up. 'Cross the ocean huh?'

Hope continued to turn the hat in his fingers.

'That's the way I heard it....Back 'cross the ocean. Back to the Home Of Our People And Our People's People...'

Everson crossed his arms, plumes of smoke spiralling their way to the blades of a fan stirring effortlessly a few feet above them. Beneath which, the men exchanged glances and searched the sheaf of paper for further details.

Hope watched as Everson drew himself to his feet and making it look like it was far from unfamiliar procedure, reached to a map hanging from the wall, pointing to a block of land – the *only* reachable block of land, across what was the only passable stretch of sea.

'Guess this is the place you're talking about,' he said, a trailing finger indicating the former home of generations of migratory Desert Settlers: a narrow neck of land across a thin blue patch at the top of the map.

Hope could only assume it was, never having been there himself and certainly never having seen a picture of it hanging on a wall in front of him before.

'There's your ocean,' said Everson, sliding his finger over the blue patch that effectively split the upper and lower continent into two distinct halves.

Hope was neither impressed nor unimpressed by Everson's demonstration; his knowledge of what was generally referred to as their 'True Home' sketchy to say the least however many times he'd been regaled with tales and songs about it back home.

'Expensive business getting a guy across the sea,' Everson said, puffing on the cigar and making his way back to the desk. 'Specially a *dead* guy.'

Oblivious of proceedings for a moment he flicked the document in his hand and set about directing conversation over his shoulder.

It was a minute or two later that he spun round in his chair, slapping the paper on the desk.

'Okay,' he said, in a tone indicating they were maybe in a position to get down to a little business.

'So, let's see what we're looking at here.' Another quick glance at the figures as he spoke. 'So that's two days in the desert, two nights in hold, transport 'cross the ocean, customs, taxes, funeral-costs...I guess we're looking at...six hundred dollars!'

Arms folded he thrust himself back in his chair, the cigar rolling unaided from one side of his mouth to the other.

There was little reaction across the desk on account of there being little to react to. No way could Hope even conceive of coming up with that kind of money. He stared at the pile of papers sitting on the desk...stuff that had barely registered since taking his seat yet stuff that evidently had far more to say about where folks were heading when their time was done than any of the stuff that got talked about and sung about on porches back home – or had been scratched on tablets of stone half buried in someone else's desert. Or at least that it was less straightforward than his pa, and others like him, had been led to believe!

He stopped – a quite different voice suddenly speaking more loudly than any voice he'd been hearing thus far. A voice telling him he was likely going to have to go back and re-think the whole thing – maybe get his pa across The Desert and aboard ship himself and work his passage that way, getting him to where he needed to be got to by hitching a ride on the back of some cart making its way home from market.

None of which escaped notice across the desk where Everson laid the cigar to one side and adjusted himself in his seat.

'More than you'd figured huh?' Shoulders hunched, arms folded, he turned the paper back into place beneath him.

'Okay. Let's come at it from another angle. How about you tell me what you was thinking and we'll see if we can maybe search these papers here and maybe come up with some way of getting your pa 'cross the ocean for a little less than we'd been looking at.'

Hope was far from convinced. Whatever deal they could come up with was sure to exceed anything he could even dream of coming up with. The only consolation being it didn't cost anything to listen, at least not yet! The idea of setting off across

The Desert with his pa slumped over a cart *was* already beginning to sound a little crazy, as his pa would likely have been first to point out. Whether he'd have been as quick to point out that getting him back to the Land-Of-Their-People was looking equally as crazy was another issue. Trouble with his pa, and all the people of their generation was they'd rarely had opportunities – or in some cases even an inclination – to lend a moment's thought to any of this kind of stuff: stuff that was actually going on around them as opposed to stuff conjured up in myths, dreams and a few half-baked promises dug out of other folks' past: stuff that, to a man, they'd been fed since the day they were born. Which, he guessed, was where all this 'burying' and 'heaven' stuff came in; getting folk – particularly *poor* folk – to think the future (wherever it happened to be or however it could be got to) had to be a whole load better than what they'd had to put up with so far!

The only time he could recall his pa having any dealings with money was going back a while when he'd kept a few chickens and done a little bartering across a market-stall in town halfway across the desert. He could still see him dragging himself up the steps exhausted from the back-breaking miles he'd had to put in and immediately disappearing into his room to stick whatever pittance he'd managed to make into a little black box stowed beneath his bed, like he felt bad about needing to sink to such measures just to put a little food on the table or maybe about how little reward he was getting for his trouble.

It was some years after his pa's trips to town had come to an end that Hope had taken it upon himself to do a little investigating – venturing into his pa's room to discover what money would likely be heading his way when his pa would be off the scene altogether. Which, the way things were shaping up, didn't seem like it was going to be too long a wait. It certainly hadn't taken long to work his way through a few piles of silver and copper (mainly copper) in his pa's box, eventually coming up with the princely sum of one hundred and twenty dollars! A hundred and twenty dollars didn't seem like a huge return for a life spent eking out an existence on the fringe of someone else's desert, but it was all he was looking at then.

And all he was looking at now – sitting behind a desk in town peering across a pile of papers, scratching his chin to give a little more thought to what few cards he held before placing them none too firmly on the table.

'About a hundred dollars,' he announced finally, trying to sound a good deal more upbeat about it than the response he was expecting from the far side of the desk.

'Hmmm....' Everson re-shuffled the papers, working his way through one sheet, then the next then back to the first, letting his eye roam the page before drawing the sheet towards his face for a closer look, eventually stabbing a finger and raising the page to Fish.

'What do you think?' he announced, leaning back in his seat and thrusting the paper in his partner's direction.

'Seems we're looking at the luckiest man in town!' said Fish, peering closer and shaking a disbelieving head.

Hope watched as Everson shuffled forwards holding one of the sheets to view.

'What we got here,' he said, pointing at a part of the page beyond vision from where Hope was seated.

'Is a...'*Cash-only – No Frills*...deal.' He made a point of indicating each line as he worked his way down the page. '*We get your folk back where your folk belong! No fuss – No Sweat – No hidden cost! What you see is what you pay*...finally thrusting the sheet for Hope's inspection should he wish to avail himself of the offer.

'You okay with that?'

Hope nodded, not entirely sure what he was being invited to be okay with but sensing they might be some way closer to getting his pa on his way back home than when he first took his seat. On completing the reading Everson looked up.

'Just a couple of things,' he said. 'Cause they do it cheap they got to make a few changes. First – they dispense with the oak casket and go for a cheaper number – you okay with that?'

Hope guessed he was. Whatever they'd be putting his pa in now he was gone didn't seem to make much difference either way.

'And...' Everson continued, the cigar rolling more rapidly from one side of his mouth to the other. 'What they do is cut out the zinc-lining in the casket. You know about the zinc lining?

Hope shook his head.

'Stops the impurities getting in,' said Fish.

Everson flattened the sheet and looked to where his partner remained stood over his shoulder checking each point as it appeared on the scene.

'Other part of the deal is...because it's a cheaper kind of wood they use and they got to put it together a little quicker, and without there being no zinc in there, what they do is – seal the lid once your pa's inside.'

'Point being – you can't get to open it no more,' Fish said, leaning closer and pointing a finger at a lower part of the page.

'You get the point,' said Everson, hopefully stopping short of needing to spell it out more simply.

It was proving quite an education for Hope who guessed he was beginning to get the picture. That once they'd got the lid on his pa he'd be sealed in – for good. Which again didn't seem too big a deal. Fact was...the guy was dead. As far as either of them was concerned – particularly his pa – there wasn't a lot more to be looking at.

'You okay with that?' said Everson. Hope nodded.

'But,' Everson said, easing himself back in his chair.

'You understand one thing. Getting him there budget price means there ain't no space for passengers; boat's too small for that. You get what I'm saying?'

The implications were again clear enough; that he wouldn't be actually accompanying his pa on the trip back to the Land-Of-Their-People, which was a shame, but at the end of the day he couldn't recall anything being said about folks needing to be accompanying their people on their way back home; and if that was the price to be paid for getting his pa back to where he needed to be got to then he guessed it was a price worth paying.

'So...' It was heads-down for a final totting up of the figures. 'Okay, I'd say that comes to...one hundred and twenty dollars! But...seeing as you done me a favour getting me to check out these special deals, call it hundred and we'll call it quits!'

Hope watched the cigar being stubbed to a small brown stump in the centre of the ashtray, its owner slumped forward. He guessed he needed, or ought to need, time to think. Everson was thinking too, only too ready to come up with a word or two of encouragement these occasions sometimes demanded.

'Think of the facts son. Your pa's dead. You want him buried, and you want him buried good. This way, you gonna get him buried good!'

The room went silent and for a moment their eyes met. The facts were plain enough...His pa *was* dead. And anyway you looked at it, that was about as certain as it got.

'Hundred dollars?' he said.

'Hundred dollars,' said Everson.

Hope turned to where the ass was peering dolefully at the building's door, its load still lying as motionless as the afternoon sun.

'Okay,' he said.

Everson reached across to take Hope's hand, Fish following suit over his shoulder. All that remained – a quick check on the goods waiting to be dispatched Gathering themselves, the three made their way into the stifling heat of late afternoon.

The ass, relieved to find itself once again the centre of attention, swished a tail and tossed a reassuring head in the direction of the cart.

Everson eased the sheet back revealing an emaciated face, still warm yet bearing the all-too-familiar pall of death.

'That your pa?' he said, leaning closer to check the extent of the man's demise. Hope nodded and gave the ass's nose a few quick strokes.

'Weak heart huh?' Everson said, looking closer.

'Could be,' said Hope.

'Maybe age,' said Fish, peering over Everson's shoulder.

Everson replaced the sheet and made for the door.

'Okay – we'll leave him there for now.'

Hope gave the ass another quick pat and followed the pair back into the building where they resumed their seats.

'Okay, so now you leave your pa with us – okay?' There'd be no argument from Hope. Schlepping his pa back and forth across the desert more times than was necessary didn't hold any great appeal, particularly at this stage of proceedings. Everson sat back a moment and shuffled a paper he had been attending to.

'Now – the question of payment.'

It was Hope's turn to call a halt. Raising a finger he took a holdall from his side and settling it on his knee loosened the tie to withdraw a small black box which he placed on the desk and reached into his pocket for a small brass key which he held to view before inserting it into the box, releasing the lid, and piling a heap of silver and copper on the desk.

The pair watched as Hope began the painstaking process of stacking the coins in small piles and easing each pile to the far side of the desk.

'Hundred dollars,' he said finally, levelling the piles of silver and copper under Everson's nose.

'Care to count it?' he said, taking a final look at what amounted to the extent of his pa's worldly wealth.

'Uh – uh.' Everson reached over and in a few seconds scooped the piles into a cotton bag held open by Fish. 'That'll get done later,' he said, putting the money to one side, rubbing his hands and facing Hope once again.

'Okay – so, now you're gonna get your pa buried, and buried good. Now – just one more thing.'

The announcement had Hope sit up once more.

'Don't know how you'd feel about this, but____'

Everson stalled, his fingers drumming continuously on the surface of the desk.

'Next week, maybe Wednesday, we got a little burial going on 'bout a mile down the road out of town. Guy from your neck of the woods, ain't that right Fish?' In an instant Fish was at his side nodding confirmation and staring hard across the desk.

'Yeh – that's right,' he said. 'Guy from the edge of The Desert, right up your own neck of the woods.'

'So...' Everson's tone dropped. 'If you'd care to come along to the little ceremony we got planned you'd be very welcome.' He pressed the tips of his fingers together as he spoke. 'No big deal,' he added. 'Just a simple ceremony for a simple guy.'

'Just doing the right thing – by him, and one or two of his people,' said Fish.

Both men waited.

Hope – keen to be seen giving some thought to what was being proposed – hesitated too, before knowing instinctively what his answer was going to be.

'Sure', he said, looking round the desks and cabinets and immediately leaping at the invitation. 'I'll be there. When a guy from The Desert passes-on there ain't no way any of us would want to miss out on that,' he said.

'Good!' said Everson, reaching another hand across the desk. 'Seems we got a deal – signed, sealed...and delivered.'

Hope extended a hand to meet it.

'Thanks,' he said, waving the offer of a free cigar away and at once reminding himself of another of his pa's favourite lines...'Never let the other guy know exactly what you're thinking!'

❧

An Afternoon With
Madam Whiplash

Connie Wallasey *aka* Madam Whiplash made her way briskly, but stepping with care, along the sidewalk. A shoulder-bag hung from one shoulder, and an old brown coat was pulled tight across both shoulders, the effect being, like generations who'd trod a similar path before her and would, in all likelihood, follow after her – she could, as and when required, slip into the comfort-zone of anonymity with every step that took her en-route to her next appointment whose address was on a folded corner of paper tucked in her right hand pocket.

She checked with her watch, pulled the bag a little higher and halfway along the next block veered to her left up the steps to a large multi-entrance door.

Minutes later and several floors higher, she reached for the appropriate button, a muffled exclamation following the ring of the buzzer and seconds later, on confirmation of the mutually arranged password, a shuffling noise and rattle of keys was followed by the door clicking open revealing a narrow, dimly-lit hallway. She made a mental note of the stairwell behind her to the right running alongside the elevator.

What she encountered was pretty much as expected: the usual arrangement of igloo-size rooms with the aromas of what appeared to be cooking-fat from somewhere off to the right.

Assured that all seemed to be in place, for the first time their eyes met.

The guy – Max – was a little on the short side, maybe five-six, five seven. Beyond which, there was little to distinguish him from any other slightly overweight, balding guy flirting with the later stages of middle-age and likely resigned to it. Plain-looking though not necessarily simple-looking, he carried what is often referred to as a paunch, and – like many of these guys who you guessed rarely left their apartments, walked in a kind of semi-shuffle in a pair of loose house-pumps, the soles of the feet designed to keep permanent contact with the floor.

Once inside and whistling tunelessly as if to convey the impression she was operating within her own four walls, she made her way to the bathroom, slipping the coat and sweater from her upper half and a loose skirt from below, checking one or two wrinkles in the mirror – a feature she'd managed to convince herself added to the effect rather than detracted from it. She smoothed hands down a sequin-studded corset and garter-belt and patted the exposed tops of thighs – still firm and coltish enough to maintain that doting motherly look – as much in demand as ever in these days of more covert on-line operations. On completing her ablutions and preparations she entered the room, her accomplice currently concealed from view at her side, to find Max already shuffling into position, arranging himself star-fish style between the four corners of the bed.

Crossing the room she took an arm, securing it with a few wraps and then the other arm. That done she seated herself on the edge of the bed to give the tethered torso beneath her a more thorough viewing.

Max too spent a moment wriggling into place, checking the bindings would be sufficient to contain him with hopefully not too much stress along the shoulder and elbow joints. After which, steadying himself with a series of deep breaths forced through hollow cheeks like a suffocating fish – he lay back staring hard at the ceiling.

Connie would bide her time; *time* as everyone in the business knew, being absolutely key: knowing what move to make, exactly *when* to make it, and to what extent; the need to read the situation; to look for clues in the guy's expression – indication they were getting close or perhaps needed to slow down a little, maybe take another check on the bindings tying him to the two top corners of the bed.

With a theatrical rearrangement of garter-belt and stocking-top and a further glance at Max steadying himself into position beneath her, it was time to make a start, the approach at this stage direct and to-the-point – almost innocent sounding...

'I saw Monique yesterday.'

There would be no response from Max who knew his role at this stage was to play dumb and stare rigidly at the ceiling, the impression – anything she chose to come out with was fine by him.

'She told me about last night.' Max was still listening but equally preoccupied in ensuring his upper-body movements would be restricted to a few involuntary jerks.

'She told me absolutely everything.'

It was the moment to have Max lay his head back, a slight puffing evident in both cheeks, lips drawn tight – reactions that didn't go unnoticed a few feet above him.

'Do you like Monique?' Again the words were delivered almost as a non-question, along the lines of some half-hearted exchange in a high-school locker-room.

'Yes,' he managed to utter, his voice scaling and dry.

'Yes what?'

'Yes – I like Monique.'

'A lot?'

'Very much. I like Monique a lot.'

'Good Max. That's good to hear.'

A finger smoothed easily along the length of garter belt, a crossing and re-crossing of her legs in acknowledgement of Max's admission. And by way of reward, reached behind to unclasp the hook of her brassiere – two matronly protuberances flopping into vision like a pair of three-quarter filled balloons.

'Now – what we need to do is, we need to establish *exactly* what happened between you and Monique right here on this bed only last night. Because...'

She paused, holding the flimsy black garment aloft for a second before letting it flop to the bed.

'I've heard it from Monique....And now I'm going to hear it from you aren't I Max?'

Max nodded. Madam Whiplash was absolutely right. He was going to fill her in on the details about what happened between him and Monique. And Madam Whiplash would listen, because Madam Whiplash was a woman, and – like Monique – knew about these things.

'So Max. You were with Monique right here in this room, just the two of you. Is that correct?'

The answer arrived in the form of another quick nod.

'Sorry Max, I didn't quite catch that.' Connie leant towards him, ears bent in his direction.

'Yes,' Max managed to utter.

'That's better Max. Lets not have any more nodding of heads, not when we're establishing what happened between you and Monique – alone together right here on this bed only last night. So...let me tell you what I heard.'

There was an instant for Connie's face to adopt a child's expression of puzzlement.

'What I heard was...you took Monique in your arms and brushed her face with *soft soothing kisses*. Is that right Max? Is that what happened? You *brushed Monique's face with gentle loving kisses*?'

The answer arrived in the form of a strange wheezing sound like a pair of tiny bellows being squeezed between Max's cheeks – eyes fixed on the solitary flex of a hanging light bulb.

'It's alright Max. That's fine. That's absolutely fine. We're just establishing what happened. So – first you took Monique in your arms and covered her face with gentle kisses. Now, let's see what happened next.'

Connie allowed her eyelids to drift, a finger hooked coquettishly over her lower lip.

'Reached for the *soft undulations of her perfectly-formed breasts* is what I heard. Is that right Max? Is that what happened – you reached for *the soft orbs of Monique's perfectly-formed mammalian protuberances?'*

A series of tight jerks was accompanied by Connie's finger hooked under a wayward strand of elastic – an attempt to readjust a garter of her right stocking and take her next cue from the figure still cavorting theatrically beneath her.

'It's okay Max, that's fine. That's good.' Her face maintained its expression for a moment, a finger pulling absently on a distended lip.

'Now, let's see how things went from there. Story goes...you then let your fingers descend – tracing their way to *exploring the beginnings of Monique's arousal.* Is that right? Is that what happened? You extended your fingers to *investigate the extent of Monique's growing excitement?'*

She looked to where Max had taken to bucking and twisting violently against the bindings – her own fingers sliding effortlessly across the metal clasps of stocking-tops, eventually closing on her accomplice still lying idly at her side.

Tightening her grip she leant to meet him, mascara'd eyelids flirting to within touching distance of his glazed expression.

'Then...story goes...you laid her back on the bed and – *made love* to her. Is that right? Is that what happened Max? You laid Monique back and *made love* to her, right here on this bed?'

Max swallowed, his eyelids clamped firmly shut.

'Tell me Max. I want to hear it from you. That that *is* what happened right here on this bed, only last night – that you laid Monique back and *made love* to her!'

'Yes,' he stammered, the word struggling for release – his head thrust back before finally coming to settle in the white hollow of the pillow.

First indications were Connie seemed amused.

'Well that's okay Max. Don't worry, that's fine.'

What followed was a five second delay, time enough for Connie to reach for her accomplice – a three foot long bull-whip complete with sculpted handle, and without a further word, bring it crashing down across Max's shoulders, its tapered end reaping huge wheals across both upper arms and collar-bones. Max squirmed – the whole upper half of his torso suddenly bathed in fire.

'It's alright Max, don't you worry – everything's fine.'

She paused only to lay her accomplice to one side for a moment; a series of light whimpering noises a reminder of a need to read the situation, to pace herself in light of developments to follow. She looked down.

'The thing is Max – did it work? Did Monique *sigh* as you were 'lacing her face' in *gentle, loving kisses*? Sounds like a couple of hens pecking in a field to me. Is that what it was like Max, you and Monique – a couple of hens pecking away at each other in the middle of a field?'

She allowed herself a chuckle whilst continuing to work her fingers over the domed grip of her accomplice *Alice* (Connie always referred to her accomplice as *Alice*!)

'And how about *caressing the soft swells of her perfectly-formed breasts*? Did that work Max? Did you manage to 'turn Monique on' with your...*gentle-searching-hands?*'

Another pause for observation whilst making a show of working her fingers up, down and around the surface of *Alice*'s bulbous grip.

'And how about...*gauging the extent of her sexual arousal?* Did that do the trick Max, worming a finger in and out of Monique as she lay *squirming beside you on the bed?*'

There would be no further reaction from Max who knew his role from this point on was to let Madam Whiplash complete proceedings in a way only she knew how. And he would listen because Madam Whiplash was a woman and knew about these things, just like Monique was a woman.

Connie turned – eyeing the first trickles of blood beginning to settle beside her gartered thighs before positioning herself to within whispering distance of Max's upturned ear....

'And how about...*making love?* Did that work Max? Did Monique moan and groan as you *mounted her* and...*made love* to her – right here on this bed?'

Still chuckling she proceeded to deliver a few more playful swipes across the bridge of Max's shoulders.

'It's okay Max. I understand.' She raised the whip's grip, her fingers continuing to explore every inch of its glistening dome.

'It's just a game. Just like this is a game: you, me…and *Alice* – the three of us spending a little time together right here on the very spot where you and Monique were alone together only last night!'

Again the smile, though cordial enough, was strictly calculated – allowing a moment for the smile to depart before raising *Alice* to shoulder height….

This time there would be no holding back. Ten, fifteen, maybe twenty strokes glided effortlessly across Max's upper torso, sufficient to have skin and beads of flesh part from his shoulders, chest and ribs like strips of bamboo. Only when her own arm ached to a point of exhaustion did she look down to find herself midst a scene that was beginning to resemble the deck of a boat on a sea-fishing expedition.

Exhausted but not quite done, Connie looked down to where Max lay unblinking on the pillow.

'You've been watching too many dumb films, reading too many dumb books and listening to too many dumb songs Max. We both know that what you did to Monique last night here on this bed was you *fucked* her…You *fucked*; she *fucked*. The pair of you *fucked*….okay? You get the idea Max?'

Max's expression gave little clue as to whether he's got the message or not. '*Fucked* her!' she said again, eyeing the crimson weals and worm-like protrusions in Max's flesh – stabbing the sculpted handle against various points on its slippery surface.

Seconds later Connie was back to her feet, eyeing the sublime look on Max's upturned face for the last time.

She straightened her garter-belt and having released the ties in each corner, reached for the bed-post to steady herself. Then, turning, headed for the door that led to the bathroom where she removed her make-up, got herself dressed, and when ready, made her descent to the street, not forgetting to pocket the envelope waiting for her in the top drawer of the bedside closet.

Before passing through the multi-entrance door at the foot of the stairwell, she did a quick count of the bills in the envelope then placed it firmly out of vision in her bag.

Back on the street there was a hint of a chill. She pulled the coat tight around her, trying to recall the next address she'd written on the corner of paper folded in her pocket.

'Jesus, it's getting cold,' she said, speaking now entirely to herself and shivering; for the first time feeling the chill biting into her limbs, no doubt indication of what lay in store for them all during the coming months.